# The Missing Presence

## EDWARD N. KELLEY

ISBN 978-1-64079-974-5 (Paperback)
ISBN 978-1-64079-975-2 (Digital)

Christian Faith Publishing, Inc.
296 Chestnut Street
Meadville, PA 16335
www.christianfaithpublishing.com

Printed in the United States of America

# Dedication

To my Lord and Savior, by the gifts of the Holy Spirit—wisdom, understanding, counsel, fortitude, knowledge, piety, and fear of the Lord—I strive to overcome human weakness, finding peace in this life with hope for everlasting salvation.

# Contents

# Preface

The story you are about to read is pure fiction. Everything written—the characters, the location, the crime, and the plot, basically everything incorporated by the author—is a figment of his imagination.

Oh, really? In religious circles, the concept or belief that Jesus Christ remains with us in the form of the Real Presence in the Eucharist has been argued by different Christian dominations for centuries. It has been said by some churches that the host is a symbolic sign or a historical representation. Others—like the Catholic Church—teach, profess, and accept the doctrine that during a Mass, a priest, through the gift of the Holy Spirit, changes bread and wine into the true body and blood of Jesus Christ.

Is that true, or is that their imagination? Why is it that some theologians say that individuals who worship evil and embrace the ways of Satan will do anything within their power to capture a host that has been consecrated at a Catholic Mass? Can you recognize Satan worship in the world today? Does a consecrated host have financial value or some type of significant importance in the world? If the answer to this question is no, then why would someone commit a murder over such a small, insignificant piece of bread?

This story unravels on a Monday morning, November 19, 1956, with the cold case murder of a Catholic priest. Sixty years later to the date—November 19, 2016—a dying man's cry for help reveals an unrepeatable mystery.

The undertone of this book may give the reader the opinion that although the author has defined this story as fiction, the facts of the story may very well describe a subtle nonfiction message. As the reader learns the facts of this case, using their own intelligence, instincts, wisdom, and good old investigative deductive reasoning, does the real question of the missing presence strike their hearts and minds? Can this story really be true?

Only you, the individual reader, can decide. Read and reflect! See if you have the ability to discern where the fiction ends and the truth begins.

# Story Characters

- Our Lady of Lourdes Catholic Church—Queens Village, New York—November 19, 1956
- Monsignor John Molloy—Pastor (victim)
- Father Frank Reilly—Associate pastor (suspect)
- Sister Mary Margret—School principal (suspect)
- Sister Eileen O'Shea—Rectory sacristan (suspect)
- Mrs. Jane Flynn—Rectory cook/housekeeper (suspect)
- Mr. Joseph Flynn—Grounds maintenance man (suspect)
- Edward Flynn—OLL student and parish altar boy
- John O'Connor—OLL student and parish altar boy
- Officer Dan O'Malley—NYC police officer (responding officer)
- Detective John McCabe—Detective, NYC police department (investigating officer)
- Mr. Patrick Walsh—Parishioner and OLL capital campaign chairman
- Mr. Walter Brady—Flynn's neighborhood friend, and active community member
- Mrs. Josephine Brady—Flynn's neighborhood friend, and active community member
- Jodi Burns—Stepdaughter of Mr. and Mrs. Brady, OLL student, neighborhood friend of Edward Flynn

- Mrs. Mary Flannigan—Administrative assistant, OLL (November 19, 2016)
- Father Jesus Cruz—Pastor of Our Lady of Lourdes (November 19, 2016)
- Mrs. Martha Johnson—Assisted-living nurse for Mr. Edward Kennedy (November 19, 2016)
- Mr. Edward Kennedy—Dying patient and storyteller (November 19, 2016)

# Chapter 1

# The Desperation Call

Saturday evening, approximately 5:00 p.m. on November 19, 2016, a call was received at the Parish Office of Our Lady of Lourdes Catholic Church in Queens Village, New York. The sole purpose for the call was to locate a priest. A parish parishioner and Good Samaritan, Mrs. Martha Johnson, was making the call.

Mrs. Johnson was an assisted-living nurse on duty that cloudy Saturday afternoon. She was an inbound hospice nurse for the hospice patient Mr. Edward Kennedy.

Mr. Kennedy, by all medical opinions, was on his deathbed. He was a lifelong New Yorker who lived a very quiet, modest life, never venturing far from his birthplace in Queens Village. Aside from an early Florida college experience, Edward was a true New Yorker.

To his neighbors, he was known as Ed, the lonely old man. He never socialized and was very rarely seen around the neighborhood. As a nighttime engineer for the Long Island Railroad, he always slept during the daytime hours and worked all night.

The neighbors, outside of saying hello or good morning, had no clue who or what Ed really was. All they knew him to be was a pleasant elderly gentleman who never married or caused trouble. Outside of some strange nighttime lights shining from his bedroom windows, he was just a nice man with enough money to have his lawn and property maintained. Alive or dead, Edward Kennedy made no difference to the neighborhood.

Ed, baptized a Catholic, stopped practicing the Catholic faith as soon as he was old enough to be out of his parents' house. Raised in a Catholic household, his parents left him no choice or personal thought on who or what religion he should follow. Catholic beliefs, Catholic schools through high school—no choice, no decision, no option, just Catholic. The one thing Ed did absorb from his childhood was there is a God! The same God for everyone was not Ed's lifelong concern. For whatever reason, he just believed there was a God.

Ed, now close to meeting his maker, was very uncomfortable not living but not dying. Mrs. Johnson, who liked Ed, suggested it was his soul that was making him very unsettled.

"Soul?" he responded. "Mrs. Johnson, God and I have not talked in forty years!"

Now Mrs. Johnson, being a spiritual woman and somewhat active in Our Lady of Lourdes, thought her dying friend Ed could use a little help. "Ed, how about I call the local parish and get a Priest to come see you?"

"Mrs. Johnson, are you kidding me? A priest? They are like doctors. They haven't made house calls since the sixties."

"Okay, fine, Ed, but if I can get him to visit, will you talk to him?"

"Mrs. Johnson, since it has been a long time since I have been in any type of church, answer me one question: does the Catholic Church still have just men as priests?"

"Ed, don't be stupid!"

"Then okay, Martha, for a $100 bet, if you can do the impossible, then out of respect for you, I will see him. You better tell him to bring a gallon of holy water because I have one hell of a story to tell him."

At that point, and without giving Ed a chance to change his mind, Mrs. Johnson rushed out of his room to get the priest's visit in motion.

The call was placed!

As the telephone rang in the parish office, Mrs. Johnson knew the odds of getting the phone answered were slim to none. Considering it was the year 2016 with a Saturday-afternoon 4:00 p.m. Mass in process or done, the office might be closed and the priests gone for dinner! Between 1956 and 2016, there had been many changes in the Catholic Church. Saturday Mass in the fifties was unheard of. It was Sunday Mass or a mortal sin.

Suddenly, the phone was picked up, and a voice responded, "Good afternoon. Our Lady of Lourdes, this is Mrs. Flannigan. How may I help you?"

"Oh, hello, Mrs. Flannigan," replied Mrs. Johnson. "I am calling on behalf of Mr. Edward Kennedy of 215th Place. I need to speak to a priest concerning a personal matter."

"I am sorry, Mrs. Johnson. Normally I am not in the office at 5:00 p.m. on a Saturday evening. The standard protocol is the answering service should take a message for a call back on Monday. Mrs. Johnson, I must follow protocol! Could you please call back and let the service take your message?"

"Mrs. Flannigan, are you telling me there are no priests available for me to talk with?"

"What I am saying, Mrs. Johnson, is I was not supposed to answer the phone and the priests cannot be interrupted at this time."

"So, Mrs. Flannigan, you *are* saying at this moment there is a priest in the rectory."

Now chuckling, Mrs. Flannigan responded by saying, "No, not exactly, Mrs. Johnson. To be more accurate, Mrs. Johnson, there are three priests: Father Cruz, who is our pastor, and two other visiting priests in the rectory at this time."

"Great, Mrs. Flannigan! I will talk to anyone of them."

"Again, I am sorry, Mrs. Johnson, but they are in a meeting, and I have been ordered not to disturb them."

Mrs. Johnson, now starting to reflect on the comments by Ed about priests not making house calls, decided to become more aggressive in her tone. "Mrs. Flannigan, this is an emergency! Mr. Kennedy is very ill and needs a priest immediately."

"I am sorry, Mrs. Johnson, but they are planning a very important healing Mass for next week and cannot be interrupted. Possibly, Mr. Kennedy could attend the healing Mass?"

Now Mrs. Johnson felt her blood starting to boil but calmly tried Mrs. Flannigan once again. "Mrs. Flannigan, let me see if I understand what you are telling me. What you are saying is there are three priests within shouting distance of the phone. Is that correct?"

"That is correct, Mrs. Johnson."

"Furthermore, you want me to tell Mr. Kennedy that I was instructed to hang up, call an answering service, and leave a message for a call back next Monday. Is that correct, Mrs. Flannigan?"

"Correct again, Mrs. Johnson."

"Additionally, and better yet, Mrs. Flannigan, I am supposed to tell Mr. Kennedy that he should figure out a way to stay alive until the healing Mass next week. Is my understanding still accurate, Mrs. Flannigan?"

"Absolutely, Mrs. Johnson, 100 percent correct! Mrs. Johnson, you got it all!"

After a moment of silence on the phone, suddenly, in a very loud and clear voice, Mrs. Johnson screamed, "Are you out of your mind? What kind of an idiot are you? I have a dying man who desperately needs help, who might die within hours, and you have in front of you three priests who refuse to have their healing meeting interrupted. You can't possibly be that dumb.

"Mrs. Flannigan, I am telling you right now, don't say another word, don't dare hang up, gently put the phone on the table, and get one or all three priests on the phone to talk to me. If they won't come to the phone, tell the pastor all five of the Johnson families will withdraw their ten children from their school, cancel all their commitments to the capital campaign, and leave the parish. Now, Mrs. Flannigan, do you understand who I am and my message for the priests?"

"Clearly, Mrs. Johnson, I will be happy to seek their counsel."

After several minutes, another voice softly said, "Hello, Mrs. Johnson, this is Father Cruz, how may I help you?"

"Father Cruz, how nice it is to speak with you. I am sorry to trouble you today, but I am calling on behalf of Mr. Edward Kennedy. Mr. Kennedy, who is one of my patients, is dying, and needs the sacraments immediately."

"Well, Mrs. Johnson, I know you and your family, and we certainly appreciate your family's support of the parish. Unfortunately, I do not recognize the Kennedy name. Is Mr. Kennedy a registered member of our parish?"

"Father Cruz, Mr. Kennedy's family had been longtime parishioners of Our Lady of Lourdes. Unfortunately, the senior Kennedy family members passed away several years ago in a terrible car accident. Ed Kennedy, several years after the death of his parents, moved back from Florida into their home on 215th Place."

"Oh, Mrs. Johnson, that *is* a terrible story. First the parents, now the young son is dying. Such a hardship the family has suffered! Mrs. Johnson, if you don't mind me asking, what illness does the son Edward Kennedy suffer with?"

"Father Cruz, truthfully, it is a combination of two factors."

"Interesting. So, Mrs. Johnson, what might those two factors be?"

"Father, alcoholism and old age are his main problems."

"I am sorry, Mrs. Johnson, I do not understand. Is the alcoholism making him appear old?"

"No, Father, he is old. I believe he is in his seventies."

"Again, Mrs. Johnson, I do not understand. I am sorry, I must be having a brain freeze tonight. How long ago did Edward Kennedy's parents pass away, and when did Edward move back into their house?"

"Father, using a round number, I would estimate approximately forty years ago."

"Forty years? Mrs. Johnson, are you telling me Edward Kennedy has been in Our Lady of Lourdes parish for over forty years and he has never registered?"

"Father, I cannot honestly answer that question, but if you come to give him the sacraments, that might be a good question to start with."

"Mrs. Johnson, if I may be so bold as to ask, how long has Mr. Kennedy been in your care, and how long do you personally know him?"

"Father, I do not understand the importance of that question, but if you must know, the answer is three days."

"Three days, Mrs. Johnson? Do you even know if Edward Kennedy is Catholic? Come on now, Mrs. Johnson. You called, terrified my administrative assistant for doing her job, then threatened to harm the church and parish for someone who you say is dying, and it is all dependent on a three-day acquaintance? Mrs. Johnson, call the answering service."

*Click!*

Hearing that horrible *click* sound, Mrs. Johnson felt an immediate rush of despair. She knew Mr. Kennedy would say "I told you so," but she also knew he was the patient, and needed her care. Without further hesitation, off she went into his room to face the music. Tiptoeing into the room, she could see Ed was sleeping and should not be disturbed.

"Thank God," she mumbled to herself. "Tomorrow I will just tell him no one answered the phone." She was turning toward the door, hoping to escape, when a loud voice called out, "Mrs. Johnson!"

"So, Mrs. Johnson, how did it work out getting a priest to make a house call?"

"Mr. Kennedy, at this moment, I am very tired, and I would really prefer not to discuss my conversation. I am confident come Monday I will have better results."

"Well, Mrs. Johnson, you now have a firsthand experience as to why people like me leave the church for forty or more years and usually never return."

"Mr. Kennedy, I am truly sorry to have disappointed you, but I really did try to help."

"You know, Mrs. Johnson, until today I never really believed in people or God, but today, your compassion on my behalf showed me there are still good, God-loving people in this world. I want you to know I really do appreciate your effort, and now, I will help you with some peace of mind.

"I promise that if you call the answering service, leave the dumb emergency message, I will not die until after the priests responds on Monday. When he responds, please give me the phone, and I guarantee you a priest will come. After all, I told you I have one heck of a story to tell him. Frankly, in all my years, I have never met a priest who could pass up a good mystery.

"Thank you, Mrs. Johnson, and good night!"

# Chapter 2

# Test of Wills

"Ah, good morning, Mrs. Johnson! Did you have a nice Sunday? How was your Sunday Mass at Our Lady of Lourdes? I assume you attended and avoided that nasty mortal sin. I'll bet there was plenty of priests in the church—you know, making sure the collections were taken."

"Well, now, Mr. Kennedy!"

"Please call me Ed, Mrs. Johnson. After all, Mrs. Johnson, the Saturday fiasco has bonded us for life, as short as mine will be."

"Mr. Kennedy, I meant Ed, stop talking like that. Only God knows when your time will come."

"Okay, fine, Martha. Is it okay that I call you Martha?"

"Yes, Ed, that would be perfectly acceptable as long as you control your sarcasms concerning priests and the Catholic Church."

"I am sorry, Martha. I apologize. I have been bitter and antireligion for so long it is very difficult for me not to criticize all organized religions."

"Ed, to answer your question, I did attend the 10:30 a.m. Mass, and it was wonderful. It was packed, and Pastor Cruz gave a beautiful homily. Frankly, Ed, I was thinking of you during his homily. He spoke of forgiveness, how much God loves us and the importance of receiving the sacraments. I prayed that God let you live long enough to receive the sacraments."

"Well, Martha, as you can see, your prayers were answered and my promise to you fulfilled. I may look like a ghost, but I am here alive and kicking. Honestly, Martha, I thought of you last night."

"What were you thinking, Ed?"

"To be frank, Martha, your personality and stubbornness is one of the reasons I never got married."

"Ed, what did you say? Are you sure you want to finish that sentence about my personality?"

"Martha, give me a chance to explain what I mean. You strike me as a woman who takes charge, doesn't take no for an answer, runs the household, pays the bills, takes charge of the children, and basically requires your husband to ask permission for almost anything and everything. In other words, you are the boss in the house and everything else in your life."

"Ed, I resent those comments!"

"That's fine, Martha, but which comment offends you the most? Before you answer, think about examining your conscience, being truthful with yourself, and try to identify which, if not all, of the Ten Commandments you have broken."

"Mr. Kennedy." Mrs. Johnson, this time, spoke in a heated tone. "Let me tell you something. I am not a bad person. My husband works very hard with long hours, so I have no choice but to be the boss of the household."

"That is very nice, Martha, but did you ever think your husband stays at work so he doesn't have to listen to you?"

"Mr. Kennedy, you are really starting to tick me off! Let me tell you something about your wonderful personality, Mr. Kennedy!"

Just at that moment, the house phone rang.

"Mr. Kennedy, I am going to answer that phone. I strongly suggest you change your attitude before I come back into this room. I am not going to hear any more of your opinions, and furthermore, when I come back, we are going to deal with your superior personality."

"Martha, 'strongly suggest'? Is that your best comeback? I can hardly wait for your return."

With that last comment by Ed, Martha stormed out of the room.

"Hello, Mr. Kennedy's residence, this is Mrs. Johnson."

"Hello, Mrs. Johnson. This is Mrs. Flannigan, calling from Our Lady of Lourdes on behalf of Father Cruz."

"Well, hello again, Mrs. Flannigan. How can I help you?"

"Father Cruz received your message from the answering service in regard to Mr. Kennedy, and he would like to speak to him."

"One moment, Mrs. Flannigan! I will put you on the speakerphone and bring the phone to Mr. Kennedy's bedside."

"That would be great, Mrs. Johnson, thank you."

Mrs. Johnson, with the phone in her hand, walked into Mr. Kennedy's room. "Ed, the call is for you."

"Come on, Mrs. Johnson, I told you I do not want to be disturbed by some pushy life insurance guy or some arrogant car insurance discount company. Just hang up on them."

"Mr. Kennedy, please just quiet down. It is Mrs. Flannigan from Our Lady of Lourdes Church calling for the pastor."

"Martha, after overhearing your Saturday conversation with that dumbbell Mrs. Flannigan and her 'I do not take calls on Saturday' pastor, why would I bother talking to either one of them?"

"Sorry, Mrs. Flannigan, I guess you heard Mr. Kennedy's response over the speakerphone?"

"Yes, Mrs. Johnson, both this dumbbell and her 'I do not take calls on Saturday' pastor heard Mr. Kennedy's response."

Now Mr. Kennedy's ghostly face turned red with anger. He was so angry for being set up by Mrs. Johnson with the speakerphone he could hardly say a word.

After a moment of silence, Father Cruz said, "Mrs. Johnson, would you please take us off the speakerphone and give the phone to Mr. Kennedy?"

"Yes, Father Cruz, I am handing the phone to Mr. Kennedy right now."

"Good morning, Mr. Kennedy, this is Father Cruz. Can we start our conversation over?"

"Sure, Father, please excuse my language! That Mrs. Johnson is sneaky and revenge filled. She really set me up!"

"Whatever, Mr. Kennedy, I was told you need to see a priest and you had some mysterious story to tell him."

"Yes, Father, that is correct."

"So what is this story about?"

"Well, Father, to hear my story, it would be better for everyone if you just came to see me."

"Mr. Kennedy, as you know, I am the pastor of this parish and a very busy priest. Honestly, I have no time for fairy tales or childish games. So please, Mr. Kennedy, tell me what is so important."

"Excuseeee me, Father—Pastor! The last thing I want to do is interfere with your busy schedule. Since I am the one that is dying, it may be best if I just took my Jesus secret to my grave."

"Come on, Mr. Kennedy, don't be so dramatic."

"Now, Pastor, dying is not the drama part of the story, you risking your soul is dramatic!"

"Okay, Mr. Kennedy, you have my attention."

"Father Cruz, what year were you born?"

"Why are you asking, Mr. Kennedy?"

"Because I need you to do some homework on your parish before you visit me. Father, please just answer the question."

"I was born in 1980."

"Father, 1980, are you kidding me? Nineteen eighty, you say? You're not old enough to be a priest, no less a pastor."

"Mr. Kennedy, will you ever get to the point?"

"Father, do you know what happened in Our Lady of Lourdes Church on November 19, 1956?"

"How could I know that, Mr. Kennedy, if I was not born until 1980?"

"Exactly, Father. That inquisitive answer alone tells you definitely need to hear my story."

"November 19, 1956? In what way, Mr. Kennedy, does 1956 affect me in 2016?"

"Well, Father, unless the doctrine and most sacred beliefs of the Catholic Church have changed in the last sixty years, you and the church are continuing a cover-up and murder."

"Oh boy, Mr. Kennedy. Could I speak to Mrs. Johnson for just one moment?"

"Absolutely, Father. It would be my pleasure to have her pick up the extension."

"No, Mr. Kennedy, I would like to talk to her privately, not on the speakerphone."

"Father, if I were you, I too would ask Mrs. Johnson privately if I was not only dying but mentally nuts."

"Mr. Kennedy, that is not what I am going to do!"

"Father, come on now, that is exactly what you intend to do. Father, it is okay, but before you talk to her and find out I am not crazy, do not waste your time asking her to tell you my story. It is solely my story to reveal, and when it comes to my story, Mrs. Johnson is as dumb as your 'Call the answering service' Mrs. Flannigan.

"Frankly, Father, since I too am very busy trying to die, don't get back on the phone with me. Just tell Mrs. Jonson whether you are coming or not. If you decide to come, check out the 1956 history of your parish. Have a good day, Father. Mrs. Johnson will be right with you."

*Click!*

"Mrs. Johnson, get in here! That was a nasty trick you just pulled on me."

"So, Ed, Mr. Wonderful Personality, did you have success with getting a priest to come visit?"

"Martha, did you really doubt my gift of gab? Of course your Father Cruz and his sacraments are coming. So what day is he coming?"

"Ed, I don't know what you told him, but Father Cruz will be here in less than one hour."

"Did you say less than one hour?"

"Yes, I did."

"That is just great."

"Ed, why are you complaining now?"

"Why, you ask? That only leaves you one hour to clean me and this dump up."

"Oh, yes. Right away, Your Lordship."

By the time Father Cruz arrived at the Kennedy household, Ed was all cleaned up in appearance. Since Father Cruz was her pastor, Mrs. Johnson was worried about Ed's sometimes not-so-pleasant vocabulary. She was starting to panic about pushing the priest-visit idea. The more she dwelled on Father Cruz and Ed's possible negative interaction, the more nervous she got. After all, Father Cruz was coming because of some unknown story, not because Ed was a good dying Catholic. If this visit went bad, her reputation in the parish could be ruined.

Just at the height of a full-blown panic attack, the doorbell rang. *Oh, God, it is too late. Please, Lord, don't let this be a big mistake.*

"Hello, Father Cruz! Welcome, and thank you for coming!"

"Hello, Mrs. Johnson."

"Father, before we go in to see Mr. Kennedy, I need to tell you he is a little grouchy and short-tempered this morning. As for his spiritual background, I have no clue. I do know he was baptized a

Catholic and he is dying. Outside of those two things, I know nothing. It was me that suggested we call a priest. So if I did something wrong, I apologize."

"Mrs. Johnson, relax, let me do my job, and let God handle whatever needs Mr. Kennedy has. Please know, Mrs. Johnson, what you did was an act of mercy and a very good spiritual gesture. I am sure God was the real inspiration behind your offer to help. Now, let us go meet the cranky old dying man."

"Mr. Kennedy, allow me the privilege of introducing the Pastor of Our Lady of Lourdes parish, Father Cruz."

"Hello, Mr. Kennedy!"

"Jesus!" Mr. Kennedy cried out in a loud voice.

"That's Jesus, Mr. Kennedy."

Again, Mr. Kennedy cried out, "Jesus."

Again, Father Cruz corrected Mr. Kennedy, saying, "That's Jesus."

For a third time, Mr. Kennedy cried "Jesus."

This time, Father Cruz enunciated his first name very slowly. "Mr. Kennedy, my name is spelled like Jesus but pronounced HEH-SOOS, not JEE-EEZUSS."

"Father Cruz, I may be dying, but I am not deaf, dumb, or illiterate. I know your first name is HEH-SOOS, not JEE-EEZUSS. I am saying the name of God's Son, Jesus, not HEH-SOOS, the pastor."

"Okay, fine, Mr. Kennedy. Let us move on past the names and get to the point of my visit."

"Father Cruz, not so fast! Do you have any idea why I am saying the name of Jesus?"

"Let me guess, Mr. Kennedy. Is it because you are at the end of your life and you need forgiveness and God's mercy?"

"That is a good guess, Father, but wrong. The correct answer is I bet Mrs. Johnson $100 a priest has not made a house call since the sixties and you would not show up. Calling out JEE-EEZUZZ was just my way of expressing my frustration with the church for costing me $100 on my deathbed.

"Mrs. Johnson, knowing how sneaky you can be, you didn't tell Father Cruz about our little bet, did you? Father, I would hate to think that you were a gambler in addition to being a conspirator!"

"Mr. Kennedy, stop being so insulting to Father Cruz. I don't want your lousy $100. I would never involve a priest in such a betting scam."

"Oh, I beg your pardon, but don't both of you get involved with the reward and proceeds from bingo?"

"Mr. Kennedy, could we excuse Mrs. Johnson, and stop playing name games and truth or consequences."

"Absolutely, HEH-SOOS, but as you will find out it is very important for me to find out how religious and trustworthy you really are."

"Is that right, Mr. Kennedy? So how am I doing?"

"Truthfully, Father, the test has only begun. Mrs. Johnson, you are excused. It is time for me and Father Cruz to have a nice private conversation."

# Chapter 3

# Story Worthiness

"Well, Mr. Kennedy, I am here. Your request has been fulfilled, and Mrs. Johnson is $100 richer. Now, how can I help you?"

"Father Cruz, let me begin by saying I do appreciate you taking the time out of your busy schedule and coming to visit an old dying man."

"You are welcome, Ed, but there is no need to thank me. Doing God's work is my privilege, and I am happy to be of service to you and the community of Our Lady of Lourdes."

"Wonderful, Father, but if you don't mind, I need to understand more about the new Catholic Church, your role in the church as pastor, and why Catholics are so obsessed, at least on the surface, with the Eucharist."

"Ed, the Catholic Church has been in existence for over two thousand years, so I am not sure what you mean when you say 'new Catholic Church.'"

"Father, it has been a long time since I have stepped foot in any church, but I was made aware the Catholic Church underwent a user-friendly reformation called 'Vatican II.' From what I read years ago, it sounds to me like the old strict church has become somewhat liberal in its thinking with a more relaxed set of rules and regulations.

"For example, you no longer go to hell for eating meat on Friday's, no more altar rails and laypeople can handle the Eucharist, and so on. Consequently, since I have not practiced since I was a kid, the church sure looks new to me."

"Ed, I get your point, but these were just minor refinements of theologian translations and not changes in doctrine. Why is this type of change so bothersome to you, and how do they affect my visit here today? Again, I am still not clear on the purpose of my visit. Did you expect a history lesson or reconciliation with God and the anointing of the sick in preparation that God does call you? Although a reconciliation is my objective, I can do both."

"That's great, Father! Father, do you feel comfortable calling me Ed?"

"If you are okay with it Ed, it is fine with me."

"Good, it is my intention to have us become friends, and I am starting to feel like I can open up to you, but just not yet."

"That is great, Ed! Does this mean we can move on to the story and my purpose here?"

"Father, we are almost there but not totally. Here is what we can do: you can ask me some introduction questions that you might need answers for in case a reconciliation does take place."

"Okay, that is fine with me. So, do you consider yourself a Catholic?"

"In name only, Father, and only when I am in the hospital and someone asks my religious preference."

"Okay, so if someone asked you if you believe in God, you would say what?"

"I would answer yes, and without hesitation!"

"Would you like to tell me what is bothering you?"

"Father, come on now. Are you trying to get me to participate in your so-called reconciliation after two simple questions? That's another thing! What happened to plain old word *confession*?"

"No, Ed, but I am desperately trying to understand what you want from me. Can you at least admit that we are going round and round and nothing is changing?"

"Father, it may seem that way to you, but you are not correct. Since you are not in the know, I will admit this all may be very strange to you. However, once you know the whole story, all the pieces will come together. What is important to me is before I begin to reveal my very important story to you, I must believe that you are grounded in your faith and your soul possesses the worthiness to receive the story.

"The fact that you are a Catholic priest does not automatically qualify you. From what I have read over the years, there are some very good priests and some who have been unworthy of God's gift to be chosen to be a priest. All I am trying to do is to get a comfort level with your spirit and your soul."

"Ed, you are making me feel like I have been selected to be a game show contestant. Did my Baptist family or some of my practical joker associates put you up to this? Are there hidden cameras in the room? Are you sure you are a dying old man and not a game show host? Give me one good reason why I should not just walk out right now."

"Your dead pastor Monsignor Molloy, who was murdered on November 19, 1956, in the rectory of Our Lady of Lourdes Church?"

"What are you talking about, Ed?"

"You wanted one reason, and there it is!"

"I don't know what you are talking about."

"Well, Father HEH-SOOSSSS, did you do the homework assignment I gave you to do before you came to see me?"

"As a matter of fact, I did! There was no such murder, and for your information, Monsignor Molloy died of natural causes."

"If you call his 'broken neck' natural causes, then you might as well leave now."

"A broken neck? Where did you hear that? In all my research of the parish, I never heard such garbage."

"Wow, Father, it sure didn't take much to get your New York dander up, and with that Spanish accent, you at least are now showing you got spunk."

With that outburst, Mrs. Johnson knocked and opened the door. "Father, are you okay? Mr. Kennedy, are you behaving yourself?"

"Yes, Mrs. Johnson, we are fine. Father Cruz had a little trouble swallowing a tidbit, so he tried to cough it out."

"Father, can I get you water?"

"Mrs. Johnson, I think your good pastor needs a stiff drink, not water!"

"No, Mrs. Johnson, I am much better now, thank you, and please close the door." Father Cruz turned to Mr. Kennedy. "How do you know this murder stuff? I am starting to think you brought me here to discredit me or for some personal insulting entertainment, or you're just plain nuts!"

"Not really, but if that is a multiple-choice question, I am leaning toward just plain nuts. It's not important how I know about the murder. What is important is the murder is just the tip of the iceberg. Furthermore, now that you have been told of the murder, you are now a co-conspirator to the cover up."

"Come on! What do I have to do with some murder from November 1956?"

"Okay, Father, I am going to give you a chance to be a church hero, a church heretic, or a coward in faith. Which one would you like?"

"What are you talking about? You *are* nuts. Who else knows about this stuff? Is Mrs. Johnson part of your scheme? Oh, dear God, please help me! This is insane."

"Father, take a deep breath and relax. I am not here to destroy you or your priesthood. I just needed to get your attention. You think you are in trouble? You probably think you're meeting with the devil. Am I the devil? No! Have I been influenced by the devil? Yes! I would concede that I may have been the entertainment for the devil for years, but I truly believe God has sent you to relieve me of a very big spiritual burden.

"Now, you sit there all frantic and nervous, but if you knew what the devil has put me through since I was a kid, you would never have come. Let me clear some things up so we can move on."

"Okay, Mr. Kennedy, but I am still confused what you want from me."

"Fine, Father, are you ready?"

"Okay, start, please."

"Yes, there was a murder. Yes, I know who the murderer was. Yes, I know how the murder was committed. Yes, the murder was covered up. Yes, the cover up was not because of the murder. Yes, all involved, including me witnessing the story, agreed to be silent."

"Mr. Kennedy, how do you know all this information? How was the devil involved, and why of all the priests in the world do you think God sent me to help you?"

"Father, all good questions, and with a little patience, it will all be laid out for you. But now I need to get back to you and who you are. First, how long have you been a priest?"

"Five years."

"Five years, and you are a pastor?"

"Yes."

"In my day, to be made pastor, you had to be one hundred years old and almost dead. You must have been part of some affirmative action program, or the church chased out everyone over fifty years old. Which was it?"

"Mr. Kennedy, once again, you are being offensive to me and the church."

"Ah, now Father, the devil made me say that. I'm just kidding! It's my NY sense of humor."

"I don't joke about the devil, Mr. Kennedy."

"Are we back to Mr. Kennedy again? I guess it's no more Mr. Nice Guy, no more trust in our friendship."

"Mr. Kennedy, friends do not treat each other the way you are treating me."

"Is that right, Father HEH-SOOSSS? You should see the way God and Satan have treated me for the last sixty years.

"Father Cruz, what is your opinion on the church's doctrine concerning the 'Real' Presence? Father Cruz?"

"I assume, Mr. Kennedy, that since you are old in your ways and have not been in church for years that your use of the term *Real Presence* means the presence of God in the Holy Eucharist."

"Wow, Father, now that is being sharp with the tongue. Anyway, that is correct, Father."

"Mr. Kennedy, it is not an opinion but my absolute belief that God is present in the Holy Eucharist."

"Father, what if I told you that the church does not possess the same absolute belief in the presence that you believe?"

"Mr. Kennedy, I would not accept that statement even if you could prove it."

"What if I told you the reason for the murder of the Monsignor was to steal the Real Presence and that the stolen Eucharist was never recovered or, for that matter, sought after? For the purpose of this conversation, let us call it the Missing Presence. Would you believe that?"

"No, Mr. Kennedy, I would not believe that. Furthermore, Mr. Kennedy, in the Catholic Church, a consecrated Host is the most important possession it has. We believe it is truly God, not a representation of Christ, as several other Christian denominations believe."

"Okay, fine, don't get your blood pressure up. I don't want Mrs. Johnson back in here. Just so I am clear, you believe personally that Jesus is present during the offertory of the Mass and the most valuable possession in the Catholic Church is the Eucharist, not all its paintings, buildings, land, etc. Is that correct?"

"Yes, that is correct."

"Considering the spiritual value of the Eucharist, do you think anyone, other than the Catholic Church, might have an interest in possessing the Eucharist or a consecrated Host?"

"Yes, I believe there are those of evil inclinations that may be interested. Now, we are getting somewhere, and you got my curiosity up."

"So you feel that the Eucharist should be protected by the church at all times, especially from those who may not be spiritual enough to understand the value of the Eucharist?"

"Yes, I believe that is correct."

"Then why has the new friendly church decided to have Servants of the Eucharist, especially in the USA, handling its most prized possession? Before you answer that, I want to clarify my point. Is it not true that the general public cannot walk into the Vatican, touch the ceiling of the Sistine Chapel, or handle the Pieta and yet the Catholic Church is friendly enough to let the generally unknown not-consecrated public handle their most valuable and precious possession, the Holy Eucharist? Don't answer that, Father. After all, that decision is above your pay grade."

"Mr. Kennedy, are you telling me that Monsignor Molloy was murdered for the specific reason of stealing a consecrated Host for purposes of evil worship? Furthermore, you are actually saying the murder was covered up and the theft of the Eucharist went unreported? In other words, the whole event was a mystery conspiracy by the Catholic Church?"

"Father, once again, let me apologize for calling you a dumbbell."

Chapter 4

# The Story Begins

"Father, I know I have hit you with a lot of questions and irritating commentary, but it is time for you to decide: stay or leave? If you walk out the door, you can just chalk our conversation up to a bad experience. As you leave, you can tell Mrs. Johnson I am not a practicing Catholic and I refused the Sacraments. Mrs. Johnson already knows I am certifiable.

"Additionally, please realize even though leaving would destroy my belief that God sent you to me, I will accept your decision. I might consider the cowardice option I mentioned before, but I will still forgive you. However, you must personally reconcile with the fact that leaving would definitely highlight the point that sainthood via martyrdom is never going to be in your future.

"Did you ever consider that unfortunately for you, my revelations, although minuscule in the scope of the whole story, has somewhat made you, like me, a contributor to the conspiracy? If no one else ever uncovers the story or the truth about the murder, you might be able to move on with your life and priesthood.

"You are young, and in today's society, accountability for almost anything is nonexistent. Besides, since I am dying, the last thing I

EDWARD N. KELLEY

want to do at the end of my life is lay a guilt trip on someone as young as you, and especially a priest."

"Mr. Kennedy, cut the crap! You know exactly what you are doing, and you know I cannot and will not leave until this is finished. Frankly, if I was smart, I would go and get a priest who has experience with performing exorcisms."

"Once again, Father, you have demonstrated the golden tongue: sharp and cutting. So does that mean you plan on staying for what Paul Harvey, the famous radio celebrity, used to say, 'And that's the rest of the story'?"

"Paul who?"

"Are you kidding me, Father? You never heard of Paul Harvey? I guess they didn't have radios in Mexico when you were a kid. Boy, is this going to be a long night!"

"Mr. Kennedy, can you do or say anything without being sarcastic or insulting? Yes, I am staying, but I could use some water and aspirins. This mumbo jumbo you are spewing is giving me a headache."

"Absolutely, Father, no problem! Mrs. Johnson, Father needs holy water and prayer tablets. Please get them immediately."

"Ed, you think this is going to be a long night for you?"

"Father, take your pills, and pay attention. My clock is ticking, and I want to finish the story before I die. Now pay attention! What do you know about witches and witchcraft?"

"Witches?"

"Just answer the question."

"Not much, Ed."

"Did you know that back in the fifties and sixties members of your parish actively participated in Satan worship and performed Satanic rituals on and around the grounds of OLL?"

"Oh, come on! You really do need help!"

"Father, you really don't think every Catholic sat around the black-and-white TV and watched Bishop Fulton Sheen every night? Do you?"

"Who?"

"God, please help me. Didn't they teach you anything in the seminary about famous priests? I'll bet you know who Gloria Estefan is."

"Yep, I know her. She teaches CCD in one of the other parishes."

"Tell me you are joking."

"Of course I am. Now who is the dumbbell? There is no way the church would allow Satan worship in the area of the church."

"You are correct, but you are assuming the church was aware of it. I didn't say the worshippers posted notices in the bulletin with a Satanic meeting schedule. Unfortunately, within the neighborhood, the congregation, even in some church organizations, evil was present. This is why I questioned you on why the church stopped protecting its most sacred possession, a consecrated Host.

"Back in the fifties, the church was totally respected, the pope was held in very high esteem, and priests were put on a pedestal and never disrespected.

"In the 1950s, normal Catholics had no real knowledge of Satan worshipers. Outside of the Bible scripture reading at Mass, to most people, the devil was a scare concept. Using the name Satan and talking about his evil ways kept the sheep in the church.

"It was not that Hollywood didn't expose the population to Satan's name with movies like *Devil's Doorway* or *Beauty and the Devil*, but the real get-your-attention stuff didn't show up until *The Exorcist* movie in the seventies. After that, everyone with half a brain knew who and what the devil was.

"But did they? People became infatuated with séances, fortune-tellers, Ouija boards, etc., but never took them serious. Yes, the devil is out of the closet but still not recognized for what he is.

Destroying families and stealing souls from God has been and will continue to be his specialty then and more so now. To understand the story, it is important that you fully understand the 1950s and how life was then."

"Okay, go on."

"In the fifties, when the murder took place, evil was there and active, but like today, he disguised himself very carefully so as not to be recognized. His best work was his ability to have an unsuspecting pride-filled soul accepting him without the individual even knowing what was happening. A simple word of encouragement from the devil or acting upon a deceitful thought encouraged by the devil, then accepted, the door was open, and the devil was in, devouring the unsuspecting soul.

"Father, are you with me so far?"

"Yes, I am."

"Okay, follow this. In 1956, OLL had a very loyal hardworking and poor family performing various services for the pastor. Their names were Mr. and Mrs. Joseph Flynn. Jane Flynn was the pastor's housekeeper and cook, and Joseph Flynn was the church and school grounds maintenance man. Both longtime parishioners with unquestionable reputations, or so everyone thought.

"The Flynns had a son, Edward Flynn, who attended OLL School and was a favorite handpicked altar boy for Monsignor Molloy. Basically, the entire family was deeply entrenched in the parish.

"The Flynns on their days off spent much of their time with their next-door neighbors, the Bradys. The friendship was natural because the Bradys had a beautiful foster daughter, Jodi Burns, who was the same age as their son, Edward. Jodi's last name was always a mystery to Edward because she was with the Bradys a long time but was never adopted.

"To Edward, Jodi's last name didn't really matter because he had a childhood crush on her, and he figured eventually it would become Flynn. Both Edward and Jodi were close schoolmates, and both were very active and popular in school. Mr. and Mrs. Brady were also very active in OLL Parish as well as being very active as community members.

"At one time I believe, Mr. Brady was a Queens councilman. Consequently, the Bradys were wealthy and could have lived in Jamaica Estates, a much-wealthier community. The Flynns, on the other hand, were low middle class. By income standards, the Flynns were poor. Unfortunately, the Flynns always had a taste for the money, but being in church services as their full-time career, the rewards were meager.

"Nevertheless, the Flynns and the Bradys were exceptionally close. How close, do you ask? They were so close that there was a rumor around the parish that Mr. Flynn and Mrs. Brady were very, very close friends, if you know what I mean.

"Monsignor Molloy, being a responsible shepherd and guardian of his parish, decided to confront Mr. Flynn about his reportedly close relationship with Mrs. Brady. So one morning, after the 6:30 a.m. Mass, the Monsignor spotted Mr. Flynn at the communion rail. As he was distributing communion to Mr. Flynn, he quietly leaned over and whispered, 'Joe, after Mass, come to the sacristy, I would like to see you.'

"Since Edward Flynn was the altar server, Mr. Flynn was surprised that the Monsignor said something directly to him at communion time and didn't just send Edward out with a note for Mr. Flynn to see the Monsignor.

"At 7:15 a.m. sharp, Joe Flynn knocked on the door of the sacristy. 'Come in,' the Monsignor yelled out. 'Hello, Joe, I have a sensitive subject to discuss with you. Wait a minute, Joe, your son and the other altar boy, John O'Connor, are still floating around the altar.'

"'Monsignor, I will look for them. Okay, Monsignor, they have left.' The Monsignor opened the conversation with the comment, 'Joe, if you are in need of confession, I will make myself available to you. Whatever help you might need, I am here for you.' 'Thanks, Monsignor, but I am in good shape.' 'Okay, Joe, I will take your word for it, but there are some nasty rumors floating around, and people are questioning if you are worthy of the position you have in the church.'

"'What are you talking about?' 'Well, some people are saying you and Mrs. Brady are having an affair. Is that true?' As Joe's face turned bright red, Joe responded, 'Isn't gossip a sin, Monsignor? Maybe you and the rest of the gossipy sheep in this parish should go to confession. Monsignor, don't ever ask me that question again! If even a whisper of that stuff or an innuendo from one of your bigmouthed parishioners gets to my wife, I will kill them, including you. Got it, Monsignor?' And the door slammed.

"Monsignor Molloy was stunned by the reaction of Joe, and was so upset he stood looking at the door for several minutes without moving. Suddenly, little Johnnie O' Connor walked into the sacristy with a smile on his innocent little face. 'Boy, Monsignor, Mr. Flynn really sounded mad. For sure, I would not want to be in your shoes if Mrs. Flynn hears that story.'

"'O'Connor! How long were you standing there!'

"'Not long, Monsignor.'

"'What did you hear, John?'

"'Monsignor, not much, only your question and Mr. Flynn's answer.'

"'Mr. O'Connor, do you know what a private conversation is?'

"'Oh yes, Monsignor, and I promise I will not tell anyone. I don't want Mr. Flynn to kill me.'

"'Mr. O'Connor, go to your classroom, and if you want to stay in this school, keep your mouth shut. Got it?'

"'Yes, Monsignor!"

"Mr. Kennedy, are you telling me little Johnnie leaked the rumor and Mr. Flynn killed the Monsignor?"

"No, Father, I did not say that. Please be patient, and stop playing detective.

"The very next day, both Mr. and Mrs. Flynn were terminated. The pastoral associate, Fr. Frank Reilly, was charged with doing the dirty work. When Mrs. Flynn—who was very upset, angry, and shocked—asked why, she was told the pastor was sorry but OLL decided to cut its budget. 'I don't understand, Father. After all these years, my husband and I have done nothing but give to this parish, and now just good-bye!'

"At that point, Father Reilly looked to Mr. Flynn for some kind of support. Mr. Flynn knew what was happening, but there was no way out. He could not share the conversation—or the rumor, for that matter—and if his wife did understand, she would never forgive him threatening to kill a priest, especially the OLL pastor.

"After what seemed like an eternity of staring at each other, Joe finally stood up and said, 'Honey, let's go. I am sure the Monsignor has his reasons. Good-bye, Father.'

"As Joe walked outside, he wondered who the Monsignor told of the rumor and his threat. He was sorry for what he said, but what's done is done. Now was not the time to reenact the conversation, the rumors, and the threats. Now was the time to just figure out how to survive.

"That night was the longest night he ever spent. Would his wife be told of the rumor? 'Did anyone hear my yelling and the death threat? I got to find a job right now. We will lose the house. If I kill myself, my insurance won't pay up. I think my best option is to talk to Walt Brady first thing tomorrow and see if he knows anyone.'

"'Hey, Walt, I need to see you. Do you have some time to talk to me today?'

"'What's up, Joe?'

"'Jane and I both got fired yesterday.' 'What happened, did you steal something?' Don't answer that on the phone, party lines! Can you come over now? It might be your answer and worth your time.' 'Walt, I'm on my way.'

"'Tonight, I will introduce you and Jane to a business group that Josephine and I hooked up with a couple years ago. They really helped me out of a financial jam. Since we met them, I have been making huge money ever since. Sometimes you might find their methods a little against Catholicism, but they will explain everything in detail. Besides, it is not like you will lose your soul. Some of their philosophy may seem dark, but the results are amazing. Just listen with an open mind, and if you accept, you will be on your way to possessing anything earthly you want. Joe, will I see you in a few minutes?'

"'I guess I have nothing to lose, so it sounds good to me. You know, Walter, the minute Jane and I met you and Josephine, I knew we were soul mates and could spend eternity together. I will be there in five minutes.'

# Chapter 5

# A Hidden Agenda

"Hey, Joe, come on in!"

"Thanks, Walt."

"I can't believe the parish and the Monsignor screwed you and Jane like that. How upset is Jane?"

"Right now, Walt, she is so angry she has not been able to express her feelings. Truthfully, we were both so stunned, and we are still in shock."

"Joe, you need to put this unfortunate setback behind you, and quickly. I believe I have just the remedy to make you realize all these past years were just a bad dream. When you look at the fact that OLL is very wealthy to just kick you in the teeth without a valid reason is pathetic. However, that is the church for you. Give to everyone in need while they have directly caused you the condition of being in need. It stinks!"

"Walt, tell me what you are thinking so I can get my mind off this bitterness with the Monsignor."

"Okay, settle down and relax. I guarantee your troubles are over. Let me start by telling you I belong to a very private group of wealthy and influential investors. As a matter of fact, I just made some calls, and they want you to start immediately."

"Walt, start what? What do you mean?"

"Well, here is the bad news and good news. The bad news is you and Jane, if interested, have to start immediately. There is no time off to sit around and get depressed. The good news is we will give you and Jane an immediate package deal of $100,000 per year to get started. Additionally, we would like you to go to Jamaica for ten days for a little vacation and a little business."

"Walt, are you kidding me?"

"No, I am very serious."

"A hundred thousand dollars is more than we made in the last two years, so what is the catch?"

"No catch!"

"Okay, what do we have to do? Murder someone?"

"No, just the opposite. We need you to protect someone and get him to help us."

"Walt, I don't understand."

"Just bring Jane over tonight."


"Honey, you won't believe what just happened."

"Let me guess, the Monsignor called and said it was all a horrible mistake and he needs us back immediately."

"Forget about the Monsignor and the church. Walt just offered us a job package for $100,000 per year, and all we have to do is protect someone and get him to help the corporation."

"Joe, he has to be kidding you. This is 1956, and no one makes that kind of money except gangsters and politicians."

"Listen, Jane, I agree that this all sounds very strange, but let's give it a chance. Walt asked us to a meeting tonight at his new house in Jamaica Estates. He wants us to meet some of the investors. At that meeting, they will explain themselves and our new job. What do we have to lose?"

"Okay, Joe, for your sanity, I will go."

Dinner was set for 7:00 p.m. sharp. Naturally, Joe and Jane were right on time. They rang the bell, and were astounded to see that Walt and Josephine had a servant and a maid.

Joe thought to himself, *What did Walt do for a living? This house is unbelievable.*

With that, Joe whispered to Jane, "I knew they had some money, but this is way over the top."

Since Walt and Josephine always went to the Flynns' house where Jodi and Edward hung out together and did homework together, the subject of their totally different lifestyles was never in question. As couples, they really liked each other so much, so the consequences of always being seen together sparked the rumors that affairs were taking place. If it were not for a series of unfortunate tragedies, the 1969 movie *Bob & Carol & Ted & Alice* might have been based on their life story.

Their children were also tight. After all, Edward had a crush on Jodi. Remember, Edward hoped Jodi would change her foster care last name from Burns to Flynn when they got older. As schoolmates at OLL, they were true chums.

Their families were great together. The only real difference, at least on the surface, appeared to be money. The source of the money was the thing that troubled Jane Flynn more than anything.

The evening went well, with lots of small talk. The only question that kept coming up as the Flynns met each individual couple was "Are you both Catholic? Do both of you believe in God?"

It seemed like such a strange first-meeting question to Jane, but for Joe, $100,000 per year was all that registered in his head. Each time he answered the question yes, the recipient of the answer seemed to have a little blank stare on the face. It was like the Flynns were being x-rayed for a weakness in their spiritual belief.

It was not until after the coffee and dessert were served when the heavy subject of employment and Walt's job offer was put on the table.

"So, Joe and Jane, what do you think of our little private group?"

Joe replied quickly, saying, "Everyone has been so nice to my wife and I that someday we hope to reciprocate the favor to the group."

"Well, Joe, Jane, I am pleased to inform you that the group has unanimously approved you and Jane joining our little enterprise."

"Walt, I don't know what to say except thank you. Both Jane and I are speechless and don't know what to say."

"Joe, just say yes, and let us move on."

Joe, looking at Jane's face, sensed the concern, but turned to Walt and said, "We are in."

"Welcome, Mr. and Mrs. Flynn! Congratulations to both of you."

At that moment, everyone at the dinner party, including the waitstaff, stood up and gave the Flynns a loud applause. Joe and Jane sat there in shock, turning red with embarrassment. It was obvious that the Flynns were out of their comfort zone, but Joe just kept counting the $100,000 for what appeared to be a simple task: protect someone and get him to help them!

*Piece of cake*, Joe thought to himself. Knowing Walt was in politics, Joe thought this was what politicians must do, and now he and Jane were in politics.

On the other hand, Jane was very concerned with the questions, the job, and the easy money, but she closed her eyes and agreed to go along for the ride. After all, things could not get much worse than having no job, no money, and absolutely no respect from the other busybody sheep of the parish. Jane, still bitter, thought, *To hell with the Monsignor!*

Weeks went by with the Flynns living a dream. Pay was great so far for a no-show, no-demand job, and Edward stuck to Jodi like glue. More and more the Flynn family visited the Bradys in their big home, and Edward got to see Jodi. Edward stayed active in the OLL student activities, continuing to be an altar boy even though he was no longer the Monsignor's favorite. He stayed involved primarily because Jodi was the nun's helper and usually attended Mass with the nuns.

The Flynn family, on the other hand, slowly withdrew from all church organizations and hardly ever attended Mass. There always seemed to be a Sunday meeting of some type that was mandatory for the little group of investors. In the beginning, Jane objected to Joe, but eventually, she attended the meeting and also missed Mass.

One evening, Edward and Jodi were alone in the family room when Edward noticed that there was not one sign of Christianity throughout the entire house. There was no crucifix, no statues, no images of saints, no Blessed Mother—just nothing. In Edward's house, at least there were signs of some faith and belief in God, even though church was being skipped.

Without hesitation, Edward spoke up. "Jodi, how come there are no signs of God in your house?"

Jodi, at first, didn't respond but then answered, "My dad likes it that way."

"I am not sure what you mean. Your family is Catholic, aren't they? Isn't that why you go to Catholic school?"

"Yes, Edward, sort of."

"I'm confused."

"Edward, stop talking stupid. It is late, your parents are leaving, and I think it is time you go home."

"Okay, Jodi. I am sorry if I said something wrong. You know I would do anything for you. Forget what I asked."

The next morning, Edward served Mass as altar boy, but there was no Jodi. Edward went to school after Mass, and no Jodi. Lunchtime came and went, and no Jodi. Edward was getting worried, and after school, he ran home as fast as he could.

As Edward walked in the door, he saw his parents were sitting on the couch with a solemn look on their faces.

"Mom, what is wrong?"

"Nothing, Edward."

"Dad, tell me!"

"It doesn't concern you."

"Why wasn't Jodi in school today?"

After thirty minutes of Edward pestering his mom and dad, Joe finally said, "The Brady family is having some personal problems. Mom and I just heard on the radio Mr. Brady is under investigation for foster care fraud."

"What? Are you sure it is Jodi's dad?"

"Yes, Edward, it is Mr. Brady."

"Does this have anything to do with Jodi? She is a foster child."

"Don't worry, Edward, she will be okay. Your mom and I are concerned how it is going to affect our family and our jobs."

"Mom, can we go over to the Bradys so I can see Jodi?"

"No, Edward, we need to stay away from their house until this clears up. Hopefully it will all work out, and you will see Jodi in school."

Several weeks went by before anyone even mentioned the Brady name in the house. It was like they just disappeared. Edward would ask the nuns in school about Jodi, and the nuns would just tell him to pay attention in class and not worry about Jodi.

Edward was getting so concerned he decided he had to see Jodi, so he took some loose change off his father's dresser and took the bus to Jamaica Estates.

"Father Cruz, are you still listening?"

"Mr. Kennedy, I am all ears. I am just resting my eyes and trying to see where this story is going. I thought you told me this was a murder, not a kid's fairy tale."

"Please be patient, Father. I am getting to a very important part of the story."

"Okay, fine, Ed, but could you pick up this pace?"

"Listen to me, Father, I am the one dying, and it is my clock that's ticking, so settle down and stop distracting me."

"Come on, Ed. The story makes no sense. I just can't see how a couple of kids fit into the supposed murder of a Monsignor."

"If you keep interrupting me, we will both be on our deathbed before I get to the end."

Silence.

"Great, Father, please keep it that way. Now where was I? Stealing his father's change and taking the bus? Right, back to the bus and Jamaica Heights!"

As Edward got to the Brady house, Jodi saw Edward walking up the driveway. She waved to him and motioned for him to be silent. By the time he got to the door, Jodi had it opened and gestured for him to come in. She immediately grabbed his hand and pulled him to the doorway leading to the basement.

"What are you doing here? How did you get here? Does anyone know you are here?"

"Stop, Jodi! Why all the questions?"

"Why, because you should not be here!"

"Well, I was worried about you, and no one would tell me what was going on. I came to help you, assuming you need help."

"Edward, my whole family is messed up. I should not tell you this, but my dad's company makes money buying and selling children. My parents deal in witchcraft and recruit others into a form of evil slavery."

"Jodi, I don't understand."

"It's true! I was sold to the Bradys when I was only three years old, along with the story I was a foster care child. I found out by accident, and now other people, like your parents, are involved with the company."

"My parents? No way, I don't believe you."

"Edward, it *is* true. I wish it wasn't, but your mom and dad joined for the money. They trade in children, not physically but by running coded ads in the local newspaper. Once your parents figured out what was really going on, your mom flipped out and tried to cancel their deal. She soon found out you don't make deals with the company or Satan and walk away."

"Come on, Jodi, my parents are good Catholics. They believe in God."

"Edward, really now. If they do believe in God, when was the last time they were in church?"

Edward, being a smart kid, it didn't take him long to figure out that his parents, fired by the Monsignor, were still angry and questioned God. What the nuns were teaching them in OLL was starting to sink in: the devil is real, and God was punishing them for the anger with the Monsignor.

"Jodi, what are we going to do?"

"Well, one option is to pay Satan back."

"Jodi, I told you I would do anything to help, and I meant it, so what can we do?"

"There is something that you might be able to do if you're not afraid."

"I will do anything to help you and my family."

"Edward, are you sure?"

"Yes, tell me!"

As Edward sat quietly awaiting instructions from Jodi, she stared at Edward as if to size him up. Suddenly, she softly said, "Get us some consecrated hosts."

"Get what?"

"Get me some consecrated host from the tabernacle."

"I don't understand. I can't do that. The Monsignor would punish me, call my parents, and I would be kicked out of school. They just taught us that the host is the real presence, the true Body and Blood of Jesus. I think that would be a big sin. I think a mortal sin. I think God would send all of us to hell. Why are you asking me to do this?"

"Why, because you are on the altar as the altar boy almost every day. Aren't you?"

"Yes, but I could get in big trouble. Why do you need a host?"

"I will explain. Years ago, I wanted something which I never thought I would get. People at our dad's company shared a secret prayer to Satan with me. They coupled the prayer with a consecrated Host, and the wish was granted. The unprotected hosts were stolen by my mom during a weekday Mass. They showed me how it works, and I got my bicycle."

"Are you telling me the devil gave you a bike?"

"Yes, sort of. There is no other way that I can explain it. Additionally, when I first came to the Bradys, they were poor. After my dad joined up with the same company that your mom and dad now belong to, they became rich and powerful, especially in real estate and politics. No one wants to lose their power and money, so it is important that we try to help. If stealing a small host solves their problem, what is your problem? Think, Edward, you could be the family and company hero. It is only a problem if you get caught, so be smart and don't get caught!"

Looking straight into Edward's eyes, Jodi said softly, "Can you do this for me? I, we really need your help! I will be grateful to you for the rest of my life. Will you be my hero?"

"Helloooo, Father Heh-soos, are you still with me?"

"I am here, and now curious."

"So, Father Cruz, was Edward Jodi's hero or coward, family savior or family goat? Are you awake now?"

"Yes, I'm thinking. That is tough for a couple of young kids."

"Well then, what would you do if you were Edward? Come on, Father, decide now, Edward had to decide on the spot. Forget you are a priest now. Be fair and go back to when you were nine or ten years old for your answer. Are you capable of being the innocent little thief or heartbreaker? Come on, Father, pick now!"

# Chapter 6

# Youthful Decisions

Early next morning, after a night of tossing and turning, Edward was awakened by the voice of his mother's calling: "Edward, get up, you will be late for Mass."

"Mom, do I have to go to Mass and school today? I did not sleep well."

"Edward, you volunteered to serve as an altar boy, and for a while, you need to stick with your commitment."

Edward immediately started to think, *Why the big push to serve? She never pushed me when they were working at the church. Now I must serve. Why?*

As Edward always did, he obeyed his mother and got dressed. Still wrestling and undecided about his conversation with Jodi, he felt really torn with stealing from the church.

By the time he walked to church and arrived in the altar boys' side of the sacristy, he was leaning against helping Jodi and the family. Once in the door, he spotted John O'Connor, who was already dressed for Mass.

"Good morning, John! What time did you get here?"

"Hey, Ed, I got here about a half hour ago."

"Why so early?"

"The Monsignor called last night and told my mom he needed to see me this morning."

"What about?"

"I am not supposed to say."

"Are you in trouble, Johnny?"

"It's not me, and I cannot tell you."

"Are you playing basketball with me later?"

"No. The Monsignor told me to stay away from you."

"What? What did I do?"

"I can't tell you."

"Come on, we are friends, tell me."

"I can't, or the Monsignor will kick me out of school."

"You, Johnny? But why would the Monsignor do that?"

"It had something to do with what I overheard the last time we served Mass together."

"Did we mess up something during Mass?"

"Ed, forget about it. I already said too much. Ed, before we serve, I want to thank you for training me on how to be a good altar server."

"Johnny, are you leaving OLL?"

"No, but the Monsignor just told me he is taking you off the schedule."

As Edward and Johnny crossed from the altar server changing room to the priests' sacristy, Edward's heart and mind were racing. *Did the Monsignor know something about my conversation with Jodi? Did someone else find out the plan to steal a consecrated Host? What should I say if the Monsignor confronts me about the whereabouts of my mom and dad? If he cuts me from the schedule, I will lose the cash tips from weddings and funerals. Why is the Monsignor trying to destroy all our income?*

"Good morning, Monsignor!"

"Johnny, get my garments out of the closet. I want to talk to Edward privately. Edward, come over here. Is your mom and dad okay?"

"Yes, Monsignor."

"Everything okay at home?"

"Yes, Monsignor."

"I have not seen them, so I was just checking. Please say hello to them for me. I miss them around here."

Edward bit his tongue but noticed Johnny was all ears. "Will do. They are just very busy with their new job."

"Where are they working?"

"I don't know the name of the company. Sorry, Monsignor, I really don't know the details. All I do know is it has something to do with moving kids."

"Oh, that's great, Edward. It sounds like they are working with Catholic charities. Please say hello."

"Monsignor, I will tell them you said hello."

"Also, Edward, before I forget, I need to tell you something important, but after Mass."

"Yes, Monsignor."

Mass went without a hitch. Edward and Johnny were both the Monsignor's favorite servers. After Mass, Edward and Johnny did their usual cleaning up and putting away the priest's vestments.

Just as they were leaving the altar boy dressing room, the Monsignor came over from the altar and called Edward. "I need to see you. John, you can leave."

"Yes, Monsignor."

"Edward, I am sorry to say this, but I have to remove you from the altar server schedule."

"Yes, Monsignor, but why?"

"Well, there are new families in the parish who attend Mass more frequently. They want their sons to serve."

"But, Monsignor—"

"That is it, Edward! I have instructed Sister O'Shea to remove you immediately."

Edward sat in the sacristy in shock, almost in tears. He loved to serve, and was totally taken by surprise by his removal.

"Father Cruz, what do you think of the Monsignor?"

"Right at this minute, I am not a big fan. He certainly could have been nicer and more supportive of the young boy. After firing his parents, the last thing I expected the Monsignor to do was dump the boy. I guess some of the old-school priests and nuns were not very pleasant."

"You guess, Father? Do you have nuns in Mexico? Brutal people!"

"Mr. Kennedy, now, now, why be judgmental? I would prefer to leave the judgment of the Monsignor up to God. It's possible he changed his ways and was nicer to Edward and the Flynns later on."

Once the shock wore off, Edward began to think about his conversation with Jodi. He remembered how she got her bike. He also remembered how the company using the power of the Hosts along with some Satan prayer got things done. He definitely did not understand the Satan-prayer part, but at this moment, he was not interested in the consequences of his actions. He was already just screwed out of his most precious gift.

Consequently, in a split second, he was on his feet looking for the key to the tabernacle. Edward knew Sister O'Shea was the sacristan. He also knew she occasionally left the key out in the open so the early Mass priests could find it.

As Edward looked around, he found it right in the middle of the counter. With one quick look at the clock, he was in action. He knew the church would start filling up for the 8:00 a.m. Mass, so it was decision time.

What harm would it be to borrow a few hosts? No one would miss them, and as Jodi said, everyone was taking them home. Thinking out loud and talking to himself, he walked to the sanctuary entrance. He saw a couple of people way in the back of the church. They were not paying attention to the altar. As was at a typical early-morning mass, the two people were just chatting away.

In one split second, and without hesitation, Edward had the key in the tabernacle, and the door was open.

Suddenly, he heard a noise in the altar boy room. Panicking, he a grabbed a whole ciborium, closing the tabernacle and returning to the priest sacristy. He tossed the key onto the counter, making a banging noise.

With the noise out came the Monsignor. "Flynn, what are you doing? Why is the bowl in your hands? Give me that right now."

As the Monsignor yelled, he reached out for Edward's collar.

Now in full panic mode, Edward quickly turned away from the Monsignor, only to have the Monsignor lose his balance and fall. There was a loud crack as the Monsignor fell, hitting his head on the base of the counter.

Immediately, the Monsignor didn't move or make a sound.

Edward just stood frozen, not sure what to do. Another door opened, and Edward, holding the bowl tightly in his hand, just ran. Once outside the church, he ran as fast as he could to his house and into his bedroom.

*If the Monsignor is alive, then Edward knew he would be dead. I need to get rid of this bowl. Where should I hide it in case they come looking for it? Tomorrow, I will go to Jodi's house and dump it. I wonder how many hosts this bowl holds.*

With that, he took the lid off. To his surprise, it was full. *This ought to make Jodi, her family, and the company very happy. I am sure if my parents find out they are going to be very upset. Their son, a thief—not just a plain thief but a thief that stole God! I can hear the radio broadcasting, "Edward Flynn and the case of the Missing Presence."*

All day, Edward hid in his room. No communication with anyone. If his parents came home, he would tell them he got sick after Mass and walked home. After all, he had asked his mom early that morning if he could stay home. She forced a sick boy to go to school. His plan was set until shortly after 4:00 p.m., when the doorbell rang. Over and over it rang!

Again, Edward panicked but decided to peek through the porch blinds. It was John O'Connor, and he looked scared.

"Hey, John, I thought you could not be around me."

"Yah, that was before!"

"Was before what, John?"

"Before they found the Monsignor *dead*. A broken neck!"

Edward, trying to look shocked and disappointed, said, "What? We just saw him this morning."

"Exactly, Edward. I am afraid they will want to talk to everyone, especially you and me. We were the last two to see him."

"Why would they want to talk to us? What did we do?"

"That is why I am here, to ask you what happened between you and Monsignor."

"Like you said, he took me off the schedule."

"Eddie, what else?"

"Johnny, what are you talking about?"

"Listen, Eddie, I saw you running out of the church with the ciborium in your hand, and one minute later, I saw your dad. After that, Sister O'Shea screamed."

"Johnny, I don't know what you are talking about."

"Eddie, this is no joke, and both of us could be in trouble."

"Why are you in trouble, Johnny? It was me and my dad that you saw."

"Because of the secret that I overhead between the Monsignor and your dad. The secret that got your dad fired."

"Johnny, just tell me what you know."

"Well, I guess it's okay to tell you now that the Monsignor is dead."

"Johnny, will you just tell me?"

Edward's facial expression changed, almost distorted looking, as John told him the Dad-cheating story. John was thinking the Monsignor continued to leak the rumor, Mrs. Flynn found out, and Mr. Flynn carried out his threat to kill the Monsignor. Johnny thought because the Flynns had not been in church they might be home fighting or getting a divorce.

Edward just sat there motionless.

Mr. Kennedy stopped the story for a sip of water. "Hey, Father, what do you think about my story now?"

At this point in the story, Edward was not the only one motionless. Father Cruz was absolutely speechless. "Mr. Kennedy, how do you know all of this stuff?"

"Patience, Cruz, I will get to that later. Let's move on, shall we?"

Edward began to realize something was wrong. His young mind was wondering. *Broken neck from the fall, my dad showing up, the affair, and sorrow for what he had done.*

He began to cry uncontrollably.

John simply said, "Edward, I am really sorry to hear about your mom and dad."

Edward, after his brief breakdown, collected himself and decided to move. *How do I get this mess under control?* Since Johnny saw Edward running from the church with the ciborium, that was the first thing to handle. After all, he didn't know the ciborium was full, and he didn't know the battle for it caused the Monsignor's fall.

Edward didn't know if his dad did come back, saw the Monsignor on the floor, and snapped his old neck.

"Johnny, let me calm you down. The Monsignor gave me the ciborium to bring to the principal, Sister Mary Margret. One of the other classes was having a Mass demonstration. As for my dad, I would appreciate that we keep this conversation quiet until I talk to my dad tonight. I am sure that by tomorrow this will all be cleared up and the Monsignor's death will be a memory."

"You are right, Eddie. I am mixing myself up, and this will blow away. After all, we are best friends, classmates, and I know you won't let anything go wrong. Now that I can play with you again, do you want to play basketball later?"

"Maybe we can play tomorrow. I am still upset about my parents."

"Okay, see you in school tomorrow. Hey, Eddie, do you think we will get asked to serve at the Monsignor's funeral? See ya!"

Shortly after 6:00 p.m., Mr. and Mrs. Flynn came home.

"Edward, I got a call from school today. Sister Margret called me to see if you were okay. She also wanted to know what time you left church after Mass. Were you in school today?"

"No, Ma, I came home after church. I didn't feel good."

"Then you don't know that the Monsignor is dead?"

"Yes, I did know. Johnny stopped by after school and told me. Dad, what happened to him?"

"They are not sure, but there were police cars and ambulances all around the church. It almost looked like a murder scene. The church sacristy was sealed off, and it looked like the bishop's car was there. Everyone knows the bishop only comes when there is a special celebration or a big problem in the parish. I guess the death of a Monsignor might get someone's attention in the diocese.

"Hey, I am starving! The Bradys invited us for dinner. What do you say we get going? Edward, Jodi also invited you, so do you feel good enough to join us?"

"Absolutely!"

"I thought so. Go clean the dirt off your face, and change your shirt."

Edward was anxious to see Jodi and show her the bowl he borrowed from the church. *Boy, will she be surprised. She only asked for one, and I got a whole ciborium filled to the top. If she wanted, she could get a hundred bikes with all of these.*

Still cautious with the evidence and not sure what was going on between his mom and dad and the Monsignor, he neatly packed the bowl in his schoolbag.

"Edward, what is that shining bowl in your bag?"

"Nothing, Ma. It's just a show-and-tell project from school that Jodi asked me to get for her."

"Speaking of school, Sister Margret also asked about Johnny. She wanted to know if he was with you at Mass."

"Yes, he was on the schedule, and we served together."

"Did you leave church at the same time?"

"I left right after him."

"Edward, are you sure? Because you forgot your lunch, and I sent Dad to deliver it to the sacristy."

Silence. Johnny was right. "He did see Dad going into the sacristy?"

"No, honey, I never saw, Edward. I got called to a meeting at the company, so I never delivered Edward's lunch."

*Why would Johnny lie about seeing my dad?*

Dinner was great as usual. After dinner, Edward and Jodi went to their basement to do homework.

"Jodi, I have a surprise." With that, he pulled the shiny bowl out of his bag.

"Edward, are you kidding me? You did it! Can I see it?"

"Here you go, open it."

As hard as Jodi pulled on it, she couldn't get it open.

"Give it to me, Jodi." Without any effort, Edward opened it.

Jodi sat in amazement but refused to touch any of the hosts.

"Go ahead, Jodi, take one and eat it."

"No, Edward, I will not."

"What are you talking about?"

"Put the lid on right now!"

"I don't understand."

"Edward, please close the ciborium and give it to me. I need to show this to my mom and dad." Just then she grabbed it out of Edward's hand and ran.

"Wait, Jodi, what are you doing?"

As fast as Edward pulled his collar away from the Monsignor, so did Jodi pull up her arm and the ciborium away from Edward. Without saying another word, she was up the stairs, and the door was closed behind her.

Stunned, Edward could not move a muscle. His only thought was everyone was going to be really mad. He could hear all the parents talking loud then laughing.

Suddenly, the basement door opened, and in a loud voice, Edward's dad yelled, "Edward, come up here!"

Once Edward was at the top of the stairs, Mr. Flynn smiled at Edward and said, "It is okay."

Now Edward was completely dumbfounded.

"Sit here, Master Edward," said Mr. Brady with a big smile. "Okay, mister, tell us how you pulled this off."

"I am not sure what you mean, Mr. Brady."

"Where and how did you get this ciborium? What is in it?"

"Mr. Brady, it is full of hosts."

"Edward, I know that whatever is in this bowl is holy, but we cannot open it."

Jodi said, "Edward can open it."

"Yes, sir, I can open it!"

"Would you please open it for us?"

"Sure, here you go." Without any pulling or struggle, this little kid just lifted the top right off.

"Wow, that's amazing, son. What is the trick?"

"No trick, Dad, I just opened it." After saying that, Edward put the lid back on.

"Give me that, son." Mr. Flynn grabbed it and tried, but he too could not open it. "Come on, Edward, what kind of stunt is this?"

"Dad, Mr. Brady, I don't know what you want me to do." With all the yelling, Edward started to cry.

Immediately, Jodi went over to calm Edward down. "It's okay, Edward, they will figure it out."

Edward suddenly had a strange feeling that Jodi was older than she appeared, and her voice was getting deeper. She was more interested in how to open the stupid bowl than how he got the bowl.

"Please tell us everything that happened today, and in detail. It is important that you don't leave anything out. This is a major accomplishment, Edward, and we just need to know who else was involved."

Edward, visibly shaking in the chair, spit out every little detail, including the conversation he had with John O'Connor. At the end of his story, he started to cry, saying, "I am sorry, Dad."

"Son, it is okay, you're not in trouble. Your Mom and I, with the Bradys and the company, will fix everything. Please go downstairs and watch TV while we talk to the Bradys."

Edward went to the basement, but this time, Jodi stayed upstairs with the adults. He could hear the parents' voices, but now Jodi's voice seemed older and much manlier. What he could make out was what the deeper voice said to his dad, "When you were invited to join this company, you were told your job was to 'protect someone and get them to help us.' I am now going to pay you $100,000 each to do just that. Edward is now under your protection. God has chosen only Edward to open the damn ciborium, and you better make sure you keep him close to you. He must not find out who I am, or you will suffer my consequences."

"Yes, My Lord, we will protect him, but what about his friend?"

"I will take care of him. Leave me now, and don't screw this up. Your life is now at stake."

Edward was now terrified. Who was the so-called My Lord that his dad was talking to? *What is going on?*

Just then the basement door opened. "Edward, come up, we are leaving. Here is the ciborium. Keep it with you at all times. It appears you are the chosen gatekeeper."

"The what, Dad?"

"Never mind. Everything will be fine."

The next morning, Edward got up and went to school like nothing happened. The sacristy was still roped off. With the way all the priest and nuns were acting, he figured the bishop must still be in the rectory.

Class started, and all was going fine until the principal came in with Sister O'Shea, the rectory sacristan. "Mr. Flynn, please come with us."

Outside the room, Sister Margret said, "Mr. Flynn, there has been an accident, and we need you to serve the Mass with the Bishop. Mr. O'Connor was supposed to do it, but he was killed this morning on his bike by a hit-and-run driver."

# Chapter 7

# Investigation Begins

"Sister, what did you say about Johnny?"

"I am sorry, Edward. We know John was a close friend of yours, and his death must be a shock to you."

"Sister, how did he die?"

"John was in a bicycle accident early this morning."

Edward just stood there without saying a word or moving a muscle. All he kept thinking was that voice saying, "I will take care of him."

"I am sorry, Johnny," Edward spoke out loud.

"What did you say, Edward?"

"What I meant to say, Sister, was I am sorry to hear about Johnny."

"Yes, it is terrible for the family, and the only lead the police have is some bystander spotted a Florida plate. Unfortunately, there is nothing we can do but pray for the Monsignor and John. Now go back into your classroom. We will get you when the bishop wants to meet you to go over the Mass procedures."

"Can I ask one question?"

"Go ahead, what is the question?"

"How did the Monsignor die?"

"They don't know yet. The police and the coroner are investigating the scene. Get back in class."

Sitting there, Edward had such mixed emotions he started to cry quietly. *I can't believe I did this. The Monsignor is dead, Johnny is dead, and Jodi has disappeared.* His biggest confusion was his friend Jodi. First she disappeared from school, and then she seemed to be someone else.

What concerned Edward even more was when he got home the night before, he asked his mom what happened to Jodi. "I did not see her when we said goodbye to the Bradys."

"She is fine, Edward. The Bradys have relatives who work for the company that live in Florida. It was planned for a long time that she would move to Florida so she could be reunited with her biological brother, who was also in foster care.

"While you were watching TV in their basement, they came and picked Jodi up. She is now going to be living in Stuart, Florida."

"Florida?"

Edward was a smart kid. Rerunning the previous day and night over and over in his head, it suddenly struck him. Gasping for air, Edward felt sick and started to turn white. Edward was in a panic attack.

*Florida relatives, Florida biological brother, Florida plate on the hit-and-run car. Oh, God, not only did I steal God, I told on Johnny, and he is dead.*

"Flynn, Flynn, stop daydreaming! What is the matter with you? Do you feel sick? Go to the nurse, now! I don't want you spreading whatever you got to everyone else in the classroom."

"Yes, Sister."

"Take your book bag with you. The nurse will probably call your parents to take you home."

"Yes, Sister."

Edward picked up his bag and walked toward the door.

"Flynn, stop making so much noise!"

"Sorry, Sister."

"You sound like you are banging pots and pans with your bag."

Edward suddenly realized the ciborium was still in his bag from the night before. He was so tired and upset when he went to bed the previous night he completely forgot to remove the bowl and hide it in his bedroom. Now he was parading around with the one thing that could tie him to the Monsignor.

*Dumb, dumb, dumb. A dumbbell now and forever!*

Before walking into the nurse's office Edward stopped in the boys' room and took a roll of toilet paper. The paper coincidentally was left on the windowsill by his dad the day he was fired. He took the paper and wrapped the entire roll around the ciborium. Before wrapping the bowl, he opened the ciborium to make sure the hosts were still there. Filled to the brim, just like before.

*The gatekeeper. I wonder what Dad meant by that.*

All protected and noiseless, Edward walked into the nurse's office.

"Mr. Flynn, what can I do for you today? What is that sweet smell I smell? I think it's coming out of your bag."

"I don't smell anything, Mrs. Johnson."

"It is beautiful and yet very distinct."

"Oh, I know what, Mrs. Johnson. My mom accidentally spilled some of her perfume on me and my bag this morning."

"Well, whatever the brand is, Edward, get the name from your mom and get it to me. It is beautiful."

"Will do, Mrs. Johnson."


"Mr. Kennedy, hold it right there! Isn't your nurse's name Mrs. Johnson?"

"Father Cruz, I am proud of you! You really are paying attention. Yes, they have the same name. The OLL nurse before she mysteriously died was my nurse's mother-in-law. She married into the Johnson family. Small world, isn't it? Any more questions, Father?"

"Mr. Kennedy, if I were to believe this story, I can't believe this kid got away stealing the ciborium and possibly killing the Monsignor. Where were the police and the diocese in this story?"

"Funny you ask that."

As the nurse was tending to Edward's sudden illness, out of the principal's office walked a uniformed NYC police officer and detective. No big deal, until coming out of the office right behind the officers was Mr. and Mrs. Flynn. Edward started turning white again.

"Edward, are you feeling light-headed? You are getting as white as a sheet. Lay down for a minute. I see your parents with the principal. I will be right back."

"No, Mrs. Johnson, please!"

"It's okay, Edward, you will be fine."

Edward thought, *It's all over now. Two cops and the bowl in my backpack! Unless they were Toody and Muldoon–type police officers, who later starred in a hit TV show, they would figure the whodunit in one minute. I am cooked! Should I run now?*

"Hi, Mom. Hi, Dad. What are you doing here?"

"Never mind that. Are you okay? Is everything safe, I mean, okay?"

"Yes, Dad, but I need to go home. I don't feel so good."

"Mrs. Flynn, it might be from the sweet perfume you spilled on Edward's bag."

"You remember, Mom? The stuff I knocked out of your hand with the bowl. You know you could not open, so I tried it, and it opened."

Looking surprised, Mrs. Flynn finally got the message. "Oh, yes, I remember now. Edward, when did you start feeling dizzy?"

"Mom it was right after I heard about Johnny."

"What is the problem with Johnny? Is he sick too?"

"Oh, Mrs. Flynn, I guess you haven't heard?"

"Heard what?"

"John O'Connor, Edward's playmate, was killed this morning by a hit-and-run driver."

Silence.

Both Mr. and Mrs. Flynn now looked as white as their son.

"Oh, that is shocking and terrible."

"Mrs. Flynn, are you okay? Now you look like Edward. There must be something going around. It is probably best that you take Edward home."

"Good idea, Mrs. Johnson."

The Flynns couldn't hit the door to the school fast enough. Unfortunately, as they walked out, the two cops were waiting for them.

"Excuse me, Mr. Flynn. Is this your son Edward?"

"Yes, it is."

"Hello, Edward, I am Detective John McCabe, and this is Officer Dan O' Malley. We are here inquiring about the sudden death of Monsignor Molloy. Mr. Flynn, Mrs. Flynn, is it okay for us to ask Edward a couple of questions?"

"Detective, Edward is sick, and the nurse just sent him home. Can this wait until he feels better? I don't think NY City's finest want to catch his bug, especially with Thanksgiving coming."

"I guess you're right, but please call me at the 105 precinct as soon as he feels better."

"Absolutely! First thing. Come on, Jane, Edward, let's get you home and in bed."

Within seconds of entering the car, Mr. Flynn yelled at Edward, "You can't be that dumb! You brought the ciborium to school. Do you think this is a joke? Do you know what will happen to you,

Mom, and me if you get caught? Stealing and murder is nothing compared to failing the desires of our Lord."

"Joe, take it easy. He has no idea what you are talking about or the pressure we are under to succeed. Edward, as your loving parents, protecting you at all cost is our main responsibility. Just sit back and relax. When you feel better, we will explain everything and get this all cleared up. Go to sleep."

Back in the rectory, there was a closed meeting going on between Bishop Sullivan, Father Reilly, Sister O'Shea, Detective John McCabe, and Officer Dan O'Malley.

"Your Excellency, I believe the death of Monsignor Molloy was not an accident."

"Detective, why do you suggest that?"

"Bishop Sullivan, I have been investigating circumstances like this for years, and when I get a gut feeling, it usually proves to be true."

"Detective, is that because you *make* it come true?"

"Bishop, I don't appreciate your tone. I know over the years we have had some differences, and maybe some police investigative methods seem unconventional to you, but our department has always been behind the Catholic Church."

"I apologize, John. I am just trying to put this tragedy behind us."

"Look, let me explain before I suggest a direction to take this case."

"Obviously, Detective, since you just called it a case, you have already made up your mind on a direction."

"Maybe so, Bishop, but just listen for a minute. The coroner came back with some unusual findings. First, the Monsignor, although getting on in years, had no physical sign of failing health. No heart attack, no stroke, no mental difficulties, no residual alcohol level, no prescription medication. Consequently, no reason to just fall.

"Second, the coroner confirmed the broken neck as the cause of death, but he noted that the angle of the head may not have caused the neck to snap. His opinion is some type of pressure might have been applied to the spine area causing a final break resulting in death. Now it is possible in moving the victim—correction, Monsignor—the examiners may have been rough and careless. However, my officer O'Malley seems to contest that statement. Dan, give the bishop your opinion."

"Bishop, slip and fall is my opinion. However, there are circumstances that cloud that opinion. For example, the key to the tabernacle was not in the place where Sister O'Shea normally leaves it. She never leaves the key out in the open. Correct, Sister?"

"Yes."

"Additionally, after checking with Father Reilly and Sister, there seems to be a missing bowl that was filled with consecrated hosts. The whereabouts of that bowl—"

"Correction, Dan, it is called a ciborium."

"Sorry, Your Excellency, I stand corrected. Anyway, for the purposes of my opinion, the bowl—until further identified—has not been located. Therefore, a possible theft."

"Sister, since you have been the rectory sacristan for years, do you agree with the officer about the missing hosts? Did you not secure them in the tabernacle with the respect the Body and Blood of Jesus deserve? Have things around here been run so sloppy that the Monsignor, you, and Father Reilly would just leave Jesus out for someone to walk away with? Is there no respect in this parish?"

At that point, Detective McCabe and Officer O'Malley looked at each other wishing they had not brought up the missing hosts with Sister and Father Reilly sitting in the room. After all, if the case went in the direction they were leading up to, the priest and the nun may become suspects.

"Well, Sister, do I need to go to Sister Margret, your principal, to get my answer?"

"No, Bishop I am quite capable of giving you the answer."

"Ready? Go ahead, Sister."

"Monsignor Molloy was a wonderful priest, and I will miss him terribly. He is not dead because we were sloppy, careless, disrespectful to Jesus or not good in our jobs. Personally, I resent your innuendos, and unlike Officer O'Malley, I know the difference between a ciborium and a bowl.

"I have never put a bowl were the ciborium goes or the ciborium where the bowls go. The missing ciborium, which belongs in and always has been placed carefully and respectfully in the tabernacle, was removed by someone other than me. Finally, all the bowls are accounted for and in the proper place.

"Bishop, Father, Detective, Officer, if you don't need me for any other housekeeping questions, I will excuse myself and return to any one of my other twelve principal-assigned jobs. Good day!"

With Sister already out the door, the bishop excused Father Reilly from the room.

"I guess I was a little hard on Sister O'Shea."

"Bishop, listen. This is very serious, and everyone's nerves have been pushed to the limit. Your Excellency, you have to admit this is not your cathedral, and having a bishop in this parish for this number of days is stressful."

"Yes, John, you are correct."

"Bishop, please, one more thing. You have to admit that nun is like what I remember when I was in Catholic school. She just chewed you out, and if she had a ruler, your hands would be very red."

"Thanks, John. So much for the NYC police department respect. All right then, gentlemen! If I may be so bold to ask, without another chewing out, tell me your direction and your plan."

"Your Excellency, this was a theft and a murder. We need to start rounding up suspects and motives. My guess would be to start with the biggest motive: the fired couple, the Flynns."

"Okay, fine, but take it easy around the parish. One of the altar boys, John O'Connor, was killed today by a hit-and-run driver."

"Good God, Your Excellency, this parish sure does have a lot of mysterious deaths. I wonder if they could be connected."

"Come now, Detective, don't even go there."

"Sorry, Bishop, it's that little gut feeling acting up again."

"Please be discreet and report back to me before the news picks it up."

"Hmmm. Little Johnny O'Connor, dead altar server?"

# Chapter 8

# Unsolved Mystery

"O'Malley, go back to the coroner and talk to him again. I want to see if he can determine the exact time of death. I will stay here and prepare my list of witnesses, motives, and suspects. With the short time between Masses, somebody had to see or hear something. Bishop, what is your Mass plan for the Monsignor?"

"John, I am not sure yet, but I intend to go back to the chancellery in ten minutes. I must notify the pastors of the surrounding parishes and the other diocesan priests. A list of invitees and Mass celebrants must be put together so the Mass goes smoothly. Additionally, I need to do some personal research on Monsignor for my homily."

"Your Excellency, if you should uncover something unusual in the Monsignor's background, you will let me know?"

"Absolutely."

"Thank you, Bishop. Enjoy the rest of your day."

"Let me see: Father Reilly, Sister O'Shea, Sister Mary Margret, the altar boys, the Flynns, and the capital campaign chairman Patrick Walsh—all might have a motive. I am guessing stealing the ciborium might have some value, but killing the Monsignor for it might be a stretch.

"I am more inclined to think the Monsignor was murdered for jealousy, revenge, or because he knew something that someone wanted to keep a secret. It might have been something the Monsignor heard in confession and the confessor realized the danger and shut him up. This is going to be a lot of digging. I think I will get the nuns over here and chat with them.

"Excuse me, Father Reilly, how can I reach the school and the principal?"

"Simple, Detective. There is an intercom in the sacristy which we use to call the principal for altar boys if needed."

"Thanks, Father. I will call them now."

"Sister Margret, how did you get along with the Monsignor?"

"He was a good priest and a nice man."

"Do you ever have any school-operating issues with him?"

"Naturally, we did not always agree on every policy and procedure."

"Like what, Sister?"

"It was always trivial stuff."

"Like what, Sister?"

"It was nothing important, just little personality clashes."

"Like what, Sister?"

"I would prefer not to discuss them, Detective."

"Sister, the Monsignor is dead, and I am investigating a theft and a murder."

"What do you mean, Detective?"

"A missing ciborium and a Monsignor with a broken neck due to blunt trauma is why I need details."

"Well, this is the first time I am hearing the Monsignor's death explained that way. I was told it was an accident. What's up with the story change?"

"Well, Sister, if you must know, Sister O'Shea reported the missing full ciborium to Father Reilly, and the bishop just blasted her for not being more careful with the tabernacle key."

"That old cantankerous bishop would shoot first than ask questions later. Detective, let me clear something up right now. First, my relationship with the Monsignor, although not perfect, was workable. Second, Sister O'Shea is a kind, hardworking sister with not a mean bone in her body. She has gone above and beyond to please me, the priests, the Monsignor, the parishioners, and the cranky old bishop. I resent the tone of your questions and the idea that would even consider accusing me or my fellow sister as thieves or murderers. Detective McCabe, we are done!"

Out the door she went, slamming the door behind her.

*Wow, another pissed-off, hot-headed nun. What's with these nuns slamming doors and walking out? I wonder if one of their training seminars includes a class called the Bristle Stomp. Get their hackles up, they bristle and stomp out of the door. Now that was not a good start. Since I have already seen Sister O'Shea rip the Bishop, I think I will jump to Father Reilly.*

"Father Reilly, would you be so kind to come and join me for a couple of questions?" Detective McCabe asked.

"Hey, Detective, how can I help you? I'll try to be more cooperative than Sister Margret."

"How did you know Sister Margret was a little short with her answers?"

"Honestly, you left the intercom on after you made the announcement to the principal."

"Okay, Father, my mistake. Are you in the habit of eavesdropping?"

"No, not really."

"So why did you eavesdrop this time?"

"Why, because that cantankerous bishop ordered me to learn everything you find out and report back to him."

"Okay, so what did you learn so far by eavesdropping?"

"I learned that I agreed with Sister Margret. The bishop *is* cantankerous, and Sister O'Shea does a great job supporting us priests."

"Did you hear anything else, Father Reilly?"

"Nope, that's it."

"Thank you, Father, you can leave now."

"Have a good day, Detective."

"And the same to you, Father. Oh, Father, one more question: is there any chance the intercom was on the morning that the Monsignor died?"

"Yes. Now that you mentioned it, the intercom was definitely on."

"How do you know that?"

"I heard the Monsignor yelling about some bowl."

"Was he yelling *bowl* or *ciborium*?"

"I think he said *bowl*."

"Could he have really been talking about a ciborium?"

"Sure it's possible."

Since the bishop made a big deal with Officer O'Malley for not using the word *ciborium*, why would the Monsignor call it a bowl?"

"I can't answer that, except to assume the Monsignor was confused."

"Fine. Now this is very important: did you hear any name or anything else?"

"I had just walked into the kitchen for coffee, and I am not 100 percent sure."

"Come on, Father, concentrate."

"I remember thinking about me doing the 8:00 a.m. Mass and the altar boy schedule. Yes, I heard the Monsignor use the name Flynn."

"Was it Mr. Flynn, Edward Flynn, Jane Flynn?"

"I am not sure, Detective. I think it was just Flynn."

"Thank you, Father. That is a big help."

McCabe briskly walked out to his patrol car and grabbed the microphone. "This is Detective McCabe. Patch me into O'Malley. Get over to the Flynns' house and pick up all the Flynns."

"Why, Chief?"

"Just do it, and bring them to me at the church."

"Mr. Kennedy, are you telling me that all the Flynns are going to get arrested for the murder of the Monsignor?"

"No, Father Cruz, I am not saying that, and you are jumping to conclusions."

"But you said Father Reilly said Flynn and then O'Malley was ordered to pick up everyone."

"Father, you really need to relax! Would you like to eat something? I can have Mrs. Johnson whip something up for us. Maybe you would like some hot Mexican specialty?"

"Don't start again, Kennedy. Are you kidding me? You have been teasing me for hours with your murder mystery, and you want to stop for dinner? I still have no idea why I am here and what this story has to do with me, so let's get on with it. I don't have much time left."

As he sucked on some oxygen, Mr. Kennedy repeated Father's statement: "You don't have much time left. Father, get real! Okay, where was I?"

"You ended with getting the Flynns."

"Yes, yes."

While all this investigating was going on, Mr. and Mrs. Flynn had taken Edward home, telling him to hide the bowl and get some sleep.

Concerned that things were unraveling, Jane started complaining to Joe that she didn't like any of this stuff and they should confront the company on what protection they had. Yes, a $100,000 each per year was great to protect Edward and the ciborium, but if they were caught, all the money in the world wouldn't help them.

Joe listened to his wife and said, "You are right. While Edward is sleeping, I am going to call Walt and get his opinion."

"Thank you, honey. I feel better already."

As Joe dialed the number, the doorbell rang. It was his cousins who lived just a couple of blocks away. Jane answered the door and greeted the cousins, saying, "Joe is on the phone. He will join us in a few minutes. Come on in and sit down. What a surprise!"

"Honestly, well, we were walking around the neighborhood, and we thought we would stop in and say hello. We need to share some information about some strange things in the neighborhood. There has been an invasion of Haitians bringing voodoo and witchcraft into our neighborhood and the schools. Have you heard about it?"

"Oh, hey, Joe!"

"Hey, guys! Jane, I just spoke to Walt, and we need to go to his house right now."

"I am sorry, but we have to leave right now. Why don't Jane and I drive you home and we can talk on the way?"

"Okay, that sounds good. Funny, Joe, you just mentioned the name Walt. By any chance is that Walt Brady who used to live in Queens Village and got active in politics when he moved to Jamaica Estates?"

"You got it. The one and the same. Why is that funny?"

"Well, a neighbor of mine, Detective John McCabe, was just telling us that Brady is being investigated for some Haiti-to-Florida child-selling ring. They suspect his company has something to do with witchcraft and some other mumbo jumbo voodoo evil stuff."

Jane looked sharply at Joe, as Joe said, "That must be another Walt. Okay, let's go."

As Walt Brady ended his phone conversation with Joe, his phone rang again.

"Hello? We got a problem."

"What kind of problem?"

"Our new members have been discovered, and I am heading over to pick them up."

"What? Why?"

"I don't know any more of the details. McCabe wants them at the church. His hunches and those little gut feelings of his are going to cause trouble."

"Forget McCabe! Call our Florida connections and tell them to take care of the problem. The Flynns should be leaving their house now. Make the call, then do what you do best. Go for a doughnut and coffee on the way to their house."

"Fine, but this call is going to cost you more for my retirement fund."

"Just make the call and solve the problem before it gets out of hand."

Just after dark, the doorbell rang at the Flynn house. It kept ringing and ringing until finally Edward heard it and got up. Still dizzy, he went downstairs and peeked through the blinds, thinking he was undetected as he peeked.

A police officer and another couple were staring back at him.

No choice, he opened the door.

The police officer said, "Are you Edward Flynn, son of Joseph and Jane Flynn?"

"Yes."

"May we come in? We have some bad news."

"Yes, please come in."

# Chapter 9

# Family Devastation

As the police officer and the unknown couple sat on the couch, Edward began to visibly shake.

"Are you okay, Edward?"

"I came home sick from school and I just woke up. I am not sure where my parents are, but they should be home in a few minutes."

"Edward, this is why we are here. I am Officer O'Malley, and these people are from child services. I am sorry to have to tell you this, but there has been an accident. Unfortunately, I must also inform you that your parents were killed in that accident."

Silence.

Edward's facial expression changed from disbelief to shock, to horror, to panic, and back to disbelief. "No, that can't be. My dad is a great driver. It has to be someone else."

"Edward, your father probably was a good driver, but he was not driving."

"What do you mean?"

"Apparently, your parents were the passengers."

"What? Then who was driving?"

"From what we can tell, it looks like your parents were driving another couple home to their house. It looks like your dad got a flat, and instead of fixing the flat, they took the other couple's car to wherever they were going. Edward, do you have any idea where they were going?"

"No, I was asleep when they left."

"I hate to have to tell you this, but the other couple was your aunt and uncle, the Kennedys. They too were also killed in the accident."

At that moment, Edward burst into tears, screaming, "No, no, no! Don't! Leave me alone!"


Father Cruz had a strange look on his face.

"What's the matter, Father, cat got your tongue?"

"Wait a minute. When Mrs. Johnson called for me to come here to visit you, she explained your parents were killed in an accident many, many years ago."

"That's correct, Father."

"Don't tell me you, Edward Kennedy, the dying man in front of me, is related to the Kennedys who were killed in the car crash with the Flynns."

"Not only were they relatives, they were my parents."

"Oh my God, Ed, I can't be hearing what I am hearing. The parents of both you and Edward Flynn were killed at the same time in the same accident on the same day in 1956."

"Yes, Father Cruz, you are 100 percent correct. You are the winner of today's game show. The only problem is this was not a game show. Are you willing to play the next round? You could be a millionaire if you finish the game and win the jackpot. Are you in, Father Cruz? Got time for a little more?"

"Mr. Kennedy, is this how you know so much of the story? What happened to Edward? What happened to the bowl, I mean, ciborium?"

"Father, I must ask one more time. Before I go on, I have to know: are you in for the rest of the story? Yes or no?"

Before Father could answer, Mrs. Johnson knocked on the door. "Is everything okay, Father? Mr. Kennedy? Can I get some snacks or water for anyone?"

"Listen, Father, since I will be checking out any day now, how about we have one toast to the end of the story?"

"What story, Mr. Kennedy?" Mrs. Johnson asked. Is that the same story, Mr. Kennedy, that you said would keep a priest's attention?"

"Is it a good story, Father Cruz? Did it have a happy ending?"

"Well, Mrs. Johnson, it is definitely a mystery, but as for the ending, Mr. Kennedy has not yet shared it. However, if I were a betting man, I would have to say a positive, happy ending does not look very promising."

"That's enough curiosity questions, Mrs. Johnson. Please go get my bottle of Jamison and two shot glasses."

Father Cruz, who was not a drinker, considered the life-ending circumstances of Mr. Kennedy along with all the mysterious deaths in this family and agreed to one shot. Choking on the taste of Irish Whiskey, Father Cruz turned white as a sheet as if his life was over.

"Come on, Father, don't worry, you will survive. Now that you know that I am related to Edward Flynn, are you worried that some evil thing might happen to you? You're a priest! Are you enough of a believer in God to face the devil? If you are not, leave now. For the last time, are you staying, or are you going? Father Cruz, your answer."

"I will stay."

"Say that again."

"Staying."

"Oh, pride never fails."

As Edward Flynn was brought into the office of child services, I was sitting on the couch in the hallway. Realizing the only family left was cousin Edward, I started to cry like baby. Trust me, Father, I could never take the news of the death of our parents as coldly as Cousin Edward did. I wasn't sure what Edward was thinking, but his crying was over. His face looked more like he was calculating odds than missing his parents.

I, on the other hand, felt like my life was ending. Where am I going to live? How am I going to survive? I am too young for work. The more I thought about Mom and Dad, the more I wanted to die. Outside of Edward Flynn, I had no other relatives.

Nonetheless, something told me to stay close to him. He had some kind of insurance policy. Something was going on because the police, this Officer O'Malley, was paying so close attention to Cousin Flynn it looked like if Edward Flynn stubbed his toe Officer O'Malley's life would be in danger.

Edward spotted me. "Hey, Ed, I am sorry to hear about your parents."

"Yeah, Edward, I am sorry about your parents."

"Do you know anything about how it happened?"

"All I know is your father was driving and my parents were in the backseat. Somehow they got caught between two big garbage trucks, and they were crushed. The child services people would not allow me to ask too many questions."

"How come, Edward?"

"I am not sure, Ed, but I overheard it has something to do with some big investigation and the murder of Monsignor Molloy."

"What murder?"

"Forget I said anything, Ed. Unless you have your own plan, just follow my lead. I know some people who owe my family a favor, and they will be very happy to help. Let's just get through the night and see what tomorrow brings."

With that, the child services staff began interviewing both me and Edward. Since Edward seemed calm and collected, and since O'Malley wanted to go home, they interviewed Edward Flynn.

While I waited for my turn, this well-dressed man and this very attractive woman walked in and went right into the office with Edward, the counselors, and O'Malley. Not ten minutes later, I was called in.

"Mr. Kennedy, this is Mr. and Mrs. Walter Brady."

"Hello, Ed, I am very sorry to hear about your parents. We hardly knew your mom and dad, but Edward speaks very highly of them. My wife and I were very close friends of your aunt and uncle. We have known Edward for several years. He was a good friend of our daughter, Jodi, who now lives in Florida.

"Since we have a big house with plenty of room, we would like you to come home with us until things settle down. Edward will be coming, and he would like to keep the family together. What do you say?"

Father, to say I was in shock is an understatement. I knew Edward knew something that I didn't know, so I tried to smile and said yes.

"Wonderful! Unless there are any other questions, we would like to take the boys home and get them some rest. Okay?"

With everyone in agreement, the happy new little family marched out of the child services office and into a big limo.

"Boys, if you don't mind, we are going to stop at your houses to pick up anything you might need or is special to you, right, Edward?"

I was not sure what the "Right, Edward?" was, but Edward nodded yes.

The next two weeks were really rough for me and Edward. Between all the funerals, O'Malley hanging around, and Detective McCabe calling Edward to the church for questions on who knew what, things were really uncomfortable.

The Bradys did everything possible to make me comfortable. Sometimes I think Edward was jealous about the way they treated me. It was like Edward had something over them and preferred not to deal with his everyday tantrums.

Edward started to demand everything, from motor scooters to expensive sneakers to limos to school—you name it, he got it. The more he got, the more they turned their personal attention to me. It got so bad that they sent me to private school, fearing that Edward might hurt me.

Edward never left Mr. and Mrs. Brady side. Me, on the other hand, only saw Edward and the Bradys on holidays and summer vacations. Even I too could have anything I wanted. There was only one rule I had to follow: never go into Edward's room without permission. Period, no explanation.

Occasionally, I thought Edward was growing some kind of strange plant. Whenever I walked past the door, there was a sweet, beautiful smell seeping out of the room. A couple of times I asked Edward, "Hey, what are you growing in there? It really smells wonderful!"

"Ah, it's just a ventilation system Mom and Dad installed."

Hmmm, it's Mom and Dad now. When did that happen? I guess I have been away for a long time.

"Okay, Mr. Kennedy, stop right there. What happened to the murder investigation and the ciborium?"

"It is funny that you should ask. About two months after the Monsignor's funeral, the bishop called Detective McCabe to the chancellery."

"Detective, where do you stand on your investigation?"

"Truthfully, Your Excellency, since the Bradys took in the Flynn and Kennedy boys, my prime source of detail has been protected by

Mr. Brady's lawyers. My access has been cut off, and I can't uncover any other witnesses. I want you to think about something."

"Think about what, Detective?"

"My gut tells me there is a murderer out there and the ciborium is still hidden locally and will eventually turn up."

"Why do you say that, Detective?"

"Let's look at the facts: One, we have a dead Monsignor with a broken neck. Two, we have a full ciborium that has not turned up anywhere, Satan worshippers or not. Three, one potential witness, altar server John O'Connor, is killed by a hit-and-run driver from Florida. Four, parents of the other altar server, Edward Flynn, crushed in a strange auto accident.

"Five, the OLL school nurse suddenly dies of a poisonous snakebite that mysteriously finds its way into the OLL nurse's office, not to mention the snake is only found in Haiti. Six, two families wiped out and one so-called neighbor, who is also under investigation, suddenly shows up and offers to take care of the two boys forever.

"If all that is not strange enough, they adopted the Flynn boy while treating the Kennedy kid like he was their favorite son. They gave Kennedy everything like they owed him something. But here is the icing on the cake: my own investigating officer Dan O'Malley suddenly retired last month, changed his name to Dan Woods, and moved to Florida. Miraculously he got a cushy bartending job at a beautiful oceanfront restaurant called Pietro's on Hutchinson Island.

"After a couple days on the job, Woods suddenly dies of a heart attack from a bite of the same type of snake that killed the nurse at OLL. Mysteriously, the snake got behind the bar and was nesting in between the well bottles when Dan reached down, and good-bye, Dan!

"What tipped us to Dan's death was a local sheriff looking for some clues to Dan's strange death, went to Dan's listed address, only to find he actually lived in an oceanfront mansion on Hutchinson

Island, Jensen Beach, Florida. In the house, they found a young Haitian woman in her twenties who claimed to be the family nanny.

"Guess the name of the young girl the nanny was taking care of?" If you said Jodi Burns, you should run out and buy a lottery ticket. As far as the local sheriff could tell, Jodi was some blood relative of Woods and the only other resident in the house.

"After the local sheriff's department conducted a brief search of Dan's mansion, they called again to tell me they also found that Dan had shoeboxes full of cash in his closet. Some of the cash was wrapped in a piece of office letterhead with a company name on it. Bishop, would you like to guess the name of the company on the letterhead?"

"Who, Detective? I have no time for guessing games."

"Okay. The Brady Group, Jamaica Estates, NY. Can't you see it all ties together? Your Excellency, something really stinks!

"Your Excellency, I would like your blessing to blow this case wide open. With your support and a little pressure on the mayor, I promise you I will find your murderer and the Missing Presence. So what do you say? Do I have the green light to push this case up my chain of command?"

# Chapter 10

# Prayerful Decision

"Mr. Kennedy, now hold on for a minute."

"Okay, Father, what is the problem?"

"Well, up to now, I have been following the story pretty good. Now, with Edward Flynn and Edward Kennedy getting mixed together, I am getting lost in the who's who of Edwards. Additionally, you continue to talk about yourself in the third person. You are the Edward Kennedy that the Bradys took in many years ago, correct?"

"Yes."

"It was your parents that were killed with the Flynns. Correct?"

Yes, right again."

"Okay then, why do you talk about yourself in the third person?"

"Good point, Father. I guess it is a bad habit I developed over the years. Getting caught up in all the family business and secrets, it sort of forced me on occasion to pretend I was someone else. For simplicity and clarity for the rest of the story, I will call myself Ed and my cousin Edward. Will that help?"

"Ed, I hope so."

Detective McCabe sat anxiously in his chair waiting for the bishop to give the green light. In light of all the facts presented,

McCabe thought the go ahead was a slam dunk—that is, until the bishop started his response with "John, I realize that you have worked very hard on this case."

McCabe knew the slam dunk just got blocked and the green light was not going to happen.

The bishop continued. "I agree, John, that this whole series of events is very sad, but I have to look at the big picture."

"Your Excellency, you are saying no?"

"Yes, John, that is correct."

"But why, Bishop? I don't understand. You had a Monsignor murdered and the most precious valuable of the church has been stolen, and you are saying no."

"I am sorry, John, but let me explain.

"First, you and the coroner have not conclusively proven the death of the Monsignor wasn't anything but an accident. Second, all your facts, although very convincing, are really unproven. It is my difficult job to look at everything that affects the well-being of the church.

"In this case, we have looked at the death, the theft, the parish and how best to protect the church as a whole. In doing so, we cannot go around insulting parishioners with witchcraft and voodoo rumors, especially the newly developing community of Haitians. Their support and their Catholic belief to have large families will mean the parish of Our Lady of Lourdes will continue to prosper.

"Additionally, they have a new capital campaign in progress, and Patrick Walsh, the OLL campaign chairman, tells me the Haitian community has made a large commitment to the campaign's success.

"Detective McCabe, on top of everything, your obsession with investigating the Brady family, based on a little gut feeling, can do more damage to the parish than you think. Mr. Brady is a very popular politician, and he is one of the diocese's biggest contributors.

"Don't misunderstand me. It's not his money—it's the fact that your evidence is circumstantial. To continue this, again with no evidence against him or the Flynn kid, would upset a lot of people. Consequently, John, my answer is no."

"Bishop, I appreciate and value your opinion, but I do not agree with you. Consequently, I feel I must bring this case to my superiors."

"McCabe, you don't understand. I have already met with your superiors, including the mayor and his commissioner. By the time you get back to your office this case will be closed. John, let's not end this conversation in such a harsh tone. I understand your disappointment, and I promise your efforts will not go unrewarded. I will pray for you, and someday, when you become a full inspector, you will look back on this case as just another one of NYC's finest unsolved cold cases. Good day, Inspector!"

By the time Detective McCabe got back to his office, the case was closed and his commander had transferred him to 240 Centre Street, NYC police headquarters in Manhattan.

Although Detective John McCabe's belief in the church may have been shaken, he did appreciate the fact that the power of the church and politics finally came to a common understanding.

Over time, and as God would have it, the Brady investigation moved to the FBI. For years they poked and prodded into the Brady Company, but again, nothing was ever proven. Even with the O'Malley death and his hidden cash, no department could sink the hook into one single person.

"Father, here is another kick in the pants: can you guess what happened to all the shoebox cash?"

"I have no idea, but somebody probably died because of it."

"Good guess! The Brady Company lawyers got a hold of Jodi, and it all went into her trust. She was allowed to stay in the house with the Haitian nanny. She had the best schools and did whatever she wanted—that is, until she turned twenty-one. At twenty-one, she petitioned the court for her trust money. Unfortunately, over the years, the lawyers stole the money and made some bad investments. She was left broke, and yes, the lawyers mysteriously died in a boating accident off Stuart.

"The last thing I heard about Jodi was she got married and was employed as a server and bartender in a highly respected first-class restaurant called the Gafford in downtown Stuart."

"Ed, whatever happened to the Jodi-and-Edward childhood friendship?"

"Edward once mentioned to me that Jodi hurt him so bad the night of the ciborium theft and the death of Monsignor Molloy that when she left for Florida without saying good-bye he never spoke to her again."

"Wait a minute. You just admitted that when you were a kid you knew about the theft and so-called murder?"

"Father, now you are sounding like the bishop. So-called? There is no such thing as so-called."

"Ed, be honest with me. When did you first find out about all this stuff?"

"Father, Father, Father, that was very smooth. Is that how they start off hearing confessions these days? To answer your question, my best guess is I started to understand the seriousness of what had taken place and who the company really was when I was about sixteen."

"The company? I thought only Edward was involved with the company."

"Father, you are jumping to conclusions. You are starting to behave like Detective McCabe with his little gut feelings. Just relax and listen.

"There is no way we could all live in the Brady house and not hear something or see something. First, with O'Malley-Woods hanging around, then Florida people, then Haitians, then McCabe, then

90

the FBI, you would have to be deaf, dumb, and blind not to hear, see something, or suspect something.

"Did the police ever bother you?"

"Nah, my real parents were squeaky-clean. They were good, honest, hardworking Catholics with only one little weakness: jealousy. They always wondered how their supposedly 'close' cousins, the Flynns, suddenly got all their money. My parents were definitely in search of some money. It would not surprise me if their death was money related.

"The truth when told it was the strange aroma that always came from Edward's room that piqued my interest. In addition to the sweet fragrance, the neighbors' kids always asked me who those people were that stood at Edward's bedroom window every night. Even with the lights off you could see two figures, like shadows, standing in the window. It was so spooky the kids used to call our house the House on Haunted Hill.

"One night, I waited until it was dark, and I looked. There they were clear as a bell. To me, it looked like they were kneeling, staring at something."

"Ed, what was it?"

"Got me, Father. I had no idea why they appeared there. I just figured it was another Brady household mystery."

"What did Edward say it was?"

"Never said, and never discussed it. Yes sir, Father Cruz, my adoption experience was a real traumatic experience."

"I thought you said you were not adopted!"

"Oh yes, Father, I meant to say foster care experience. I am getting so weak from the meds I am starting to lose my concentration. Let me please move on. I need to finish the story.

"As Edward and I reached our college years, Mom and Dad Brady decided it would be good that we go to the same college. They also decided that we should go away to school. Naturally, with all their connections, they picked a school in Florida.

"I was not happy about that. I wanted to go to school in NY. This caused a big household battle, but I eventually won out, somewhat. How? Because when my parents were killed, our house in Queens Village was paid off by the insurance. I inherited the house, but like Jodi, I could not touch anything until I was twenty-one.

"So I agreed to go to the college they picked for Edward and me for two years, in exchange that the company lawyers get me my inheritance at the age of nineteen years. You might say a fifty-fifty settlement: two years Florida schools, then two years NY schools.

"The big kicker here was I could move back into my old house. Since the Bradys always wanted to please me, the Bradys agreed. Even Edward was happy with the deal. After slipping and telling me about that fate-filled day in November 1956, he never really trusted me. Edward wanted to get rid of me, but the Bradys would have no part of it. Consequently, the next best thing was to separate us after two years of college.

"Just before college started, I found out that the school notified the Bradys that Edward and I were to be roommates. I was not pleased with this, but there was no choice. Apparently, the Bradys got some special-donation deal, plus the school overlooked Edward's poor grades. The Bradys claimed it was due to lack of space when in actuality it was a school recommendation. The college wanted to minimize moving rooms in case Edward flunked out. Off we went to our new two-year home, me with clothes and Edward with his private secret."

# Chapter 11

# Dealing with Satan

Living in Florida was a nightmare for me. Actually, I would call it a living hell. From the beginning of school, Edward was out of control. We weren't in Florida a month when all these weird people started coming around. It really got ugly when they started to talk to Edward like he had some kind of power over them. It was like Edward possessed them, or he had some possession that they wanted to see and touch.

Edward played his part like he was a lord, or very close to being a lord. Day and night there was always some strange dude or some hot-looking woman always at the door or by his side.

Our room was a constant source of energy. Some said it was the sweet aroma that was always present. Others said it was Edward giving off a strange aura that made people do crazy things. Around campus, Edward controlled everything. No one did anything without consulting Edward. This applied to faculty as well as students. It was like he had a little secret on everyone. They all treated him with a form of respect, but I knew it was fear.

Edward terrified the entire student body. He could talk them into doing things no matter how strange or evil they may have been. Edward himself had become Satanlike. It was really strange to me.

He never studied or went to class but always got As. No Bs, Cs, Ds, or Fs, only As. I killed myself studying, and I was the one failing. It looked like I was the one who would flunk out.

One day, Edward, seeing me stress out before an exam, said to me, "Don't worry, we came to this place as a package deal, and my mom and dad will not let anything happen to you. I am their adopted son, but you are their conscience."

With that Fr. Cruz gestured by saying: "What Conscience? Come on, Ed, after all you said about the Bradys, what conscience could they possibly have?"

"Based on this story, everyone around the Bradys and the company mysteriously died. What did Edward mean by you are their conscience?"

"Father, when Edward said that, I was as confused as you are. I really did not understand the point he was making. If I was to guess, I would say the intended meaning would be I was the Bradys' favorite.

"Edward really hated me for the love and protection I received from the Bradys, his adopted parents. They liked me and felt sorry for me because of my parents. I can only describe it as good—me— and evil—Edward. I could never say that out loud because Edward was always very jealous of me."

"By the way, Ed, you keeping talking about the Bradys company, but you never mentioned the name of their company. What was the name of the company?"

"To this moment, I have kept the company name confidential."

"Why is that?"

"To protect you, Fr. Jose Cruz! The company still exists, and over the years has grown tremendously both internationally and politically. If they knew we were having this conversation, your life might be in danger. For now, I need to leave the subject of your endangerment unanswered."

"Okay, but can you at least tell me the company name?"

"Not yet, Father. Before I give up the company name, I need to know more about spiritual strength and your trust in God. Again, let me finish the story."

Our two years together never helped our relationship. Edward and I had nothing in common. He drank, did drugs, and smoked heavy. I never had any of those bad habits. Edward always engaged in one-night stands. I, on the other hand, was a virgin at the end of the two years. As I said, we were as opposite as any two people could get.

Ironically, as addictive and uncompromising as Edward's personality was, he was without a doubt the most popular individual everywhere he went. My claim to fame was I was Edward's cousin. The word around town was "Don't mess with Ed, or you will have to deal with Edward." Lucky me—it felt like I was Satan's cousin!

The two years of college flew by. Edward decided to stay in Florida, and I was determined to move back to New York. This was all previously agreed upon, and the Bradys were not the type of people that would break a promise to me.

Two months before our separation date and my return to NY, things really heated up for the Bradys. The FBI was putting lots of pressure on them and the company. They were suspected of murder, money laundering, kidnapping, child slavery, fraud, lying to a grand jury, and the list went on.

Privately, one night, Edward shared with me that the company was becoming very unhappy with the Brady leadership. The way he told me was like he was testing me, and watched how I would react to the negative Brady comment. How he knew all this was a mystery to me.

As Edward drank more and more, he revealed more and more about the workings of the company and the company's contemplation to change leadership. I told him I did not want to hear anymore.

Taken aback by my refusal to listen, his face became almost distorted with anger so much so that I became afraid, and I left the room without saying another word.

For the next two months, we hardly talked at all. Edward continuously had meetings in his room, but these meetings appeared to be with company employees and not school related. One night, I was sleeping soundly in my room when Edward violently pushed opened my door. "Ed, wake up now! I have bad news!"

I was shocked when Edward told me he received a private phone call from the company that his adopted parents, the Bradys, disappeared in a reported plane incident over the Bermuda Triangle.

He continued, "The FBI will be coming to talk to you. If they get to you before we take care of things, you must never discuss Mom and Dad's business, the company, or my unfortunate 1956 incident at OLL. Do you understand? Ed, do you understand! Look at me and tell me you understand!"

"Yes, Edward, I understand."

Father Cruz, with that bit of shocking news, Edward looked more aggravated than upset with his parents' disappearance. As I sat there in shock, Edward went into my closet and pulled out a suitcase, throwing it on my bed. "Get up, fill this bag, you are leaving for New York tonight!"

I started to say some choice words to Edward as he walked out of my room. Before the door closed, two big guys—I could only assume company employees—walked in, grabbed my bag, and started throwing my clothes into it.

"Wait a minute, what do you think you are doing?" I said.

"Listen, kid, it's your clothes or you in this suitcase. It doesn't matter to us, but you are leaving for NY within the next fifteen minutes. The boss says you are going, you are going!"

"Boss? What boss? Who are you talking about? Who is the boss?"

"Shut up, kid. With the Bradys' disappearance, Edward is now the company boss. He runs the company!"

"What? Edward, my cousin Edward, is the boss?"

"You got it, kid. Now move!"

In a matter of a few minutes, Edward went from being a dumb pothead to running a big international company. I went from being asleep to almost getting stuffed into a suitcase. Father, now I ask you, who really was smarter, Edward or me?

Packed, driven to the airport, and put on the corporate jet, I was back in NY before the sun came up. During the flight, I had some time to reflect on everything that had happened over the previous two years. I suddenly realized that Edward had been playing everyone for fools and that he was the boss. With or without his parents' disappearance, he was the designated boss-to-be. It just came sooner rather than later.

I missed the Bradys, but now I realized my protection was gone. I was at the mercy of my dear loving cousin Edward and the company. My agreement with the Bradys, arguing with Edward for two years, coupled with my knowledge of Edward's November 1956 incident and the ciborium filled with consecrated hosts, made me a candidate for burial under some football stadium under construction, or a no-return offshore fishing trip.

Panic set in. Think, man, think!

No choice. I have to suck up to Edward, treat him like my lord, and work my way out of this mess.

"Okay, kid, I am taking you to the family house in Jamaica Estates. Edward says you are to stay put and see no one until he gets here. Got it?"

"Yes, I got it."

Forty-eight hours went by, and I saw absolutely not one other person other than the two big escorts from Florida. During my detention and forty-eight–hour waiting time, serious-looking guys in suits came to the door. With my movements restricted to the basement, I could only see the company guys turning them away.

Remembering that Edward told me the FBI would be looking for us, I could only assume the serious guys were the FBI. Remembering that alone, I was fine hiding in the basement! Myself, being guilty of nothing, I did have secondhand knowledge of family matters, especially Edward's youthful crimes.

In all probability, with all the time that had passed, the FBI would have no interest in a closed case from a local Catholic Church. What was even better was no one would recognize me—or Edward, for that matter. Neither one of us had been in Queens Village or Jamaica Estates for years. Outside of the accident involving both our parents, we were unknown individuals. No police records, no identification with pictures, no fingerprints. Basically to the local community, Edward and I were interchangeable.

I often wondered why Edward was so camera shy. In Florida, he never let anyone take a picture of him, and no one wanted a picture of me. Reflecting, I now realized I knew nothing about my cousin or his motives. All I really knew was he never left the ciborium out of sight. Anyone who did see it, asked about it, or tried to open it fell upon hard times.

Once Edward knew anyone had an encounter with the ciborium, they were a danger to him. I didn't always see the consequences, but I knew they were in trouble. After all, Edward, by his action of the theft, had become the "gatekeeper," but I was never sure if he was a gatekeeper for God or Satan. All I knew was he was the only one who could open the ciborium, and if he tried to remove one host, all would disappear right in front of you. I could not believe my eyes the first time I witnessed him opening it and attempting to remove one. Poof, they all vanished.

It was like God or something forced him to keep the ciborium, allowing him to see and smell the hosts but not touch them. At one point, Edward mentioned to me that hiding the ciborium was God's little joke on Satan. God was teaching a young boy the significance of what he had done by forcing him to keep and hide the ciborium. At the same time, God protected the contents from those who intended harm to it.

Finally, after what seemed like eternity, Edward opened the basement door and came downstairs. "I guess you are a little confused with everything that has been happening over the last couple of days."

"Yes, boss. Bet your ass boss I *am* confused. Not only am I confused, I am really pissed at you! Were you behind Mom and Dad's disappearance? It seems like everyone around you mysteriously dies or disappears."

"Ed, I think you are overreacting. No, I had nothing to do with Mom and Dad, and you're still here, aren't you? We need to talk because things are going to heat up real fast, and I, as well as the company, need to know if you can be trusted. It is very important that you answer me straight. Don't get clever and try to suck up to me. My position with the company carries very heavy soul-searching responsibilities, and your answers will determine your future."

"Give me a break, Edward! You have not liked me from day 1."

"Cousin Ed, now that is a good start. If it wasn't for the fact that my mom and dad felt sorry for you and wanted you protected, I would not be standing here listening to your whiny garbage."

"Protected? What do you mean *protected*? Protected from who and what?"

"Ed, now this is going to hurt. The answer is, protect you from yourself. My adopted parents knew it. My natural parents knew it. *Your* parents knew it. Everyone but you knew it."

"Knew what?"

"That you really want to be me!"

"Excuse me?"

"You are weak, easily lead, self-centered, and destined to fail as a soul-searching fallen-away Catholic. You have no spirit or intelligence to survive on your own. You trust no one, including God.

"Without me, my protection, and the company, your life would be drugs, alcohol, and broken relationships. It was easy to introduce evil into your life. Don't make that face at me! If you don't think so, I am going to tell you some hard, cold facts. Once you understand what we know about you, you might be able to comprehend your future. Let's start simple.

"How many times have you seen the ciborium? I told you whatever God's plan was for the ciborium, joke or not, I was the only one able to open it. Evil was never allowed to touch the Body of Christ. The company kept me around strictly because I am the only living soul in the company who can open the bowl. Evil's desire is to desecrate all the hosts—that is, if they could touch them.

"Satan was very pleased with my theft as a kid. Contrary to the bishop who stopped the pursuit of the ciborium for political reasons, Satan knows what I possess. Opening the ciborium and having the Hosts disappear is my punishment and a smack at Satan. Until God feels His son is respected and safe, except for my punishment, we believe only a truly blessed person can open it."

"Are you that truly blessed person? I don't think so."

"Who do you think those images seen in my room every night were, ghosts? You saw them. What is your guess?"

"Edward, I have no idea, but get to the point."

"They were guardian angels sent to protect the Son of God. Only evil can see them. You did see them, correct? You cannot open the ciborium, correct? If you do believe in the Real Presence, what have you done to protect Jesus? What did you do to protect the ciborium filled with consecrated hosts? Nothing, zero! You are as guilty as the rest of us.

"In all these years, did you ever once think about what I have in my possession? Did you ever pray for its safe return to the church or for its safekeeping? Ed, Ed, Ed, tell me, what do you believe in? We are the company, damned forever. The company will give you just what you want, its rewards and the consequences."

# Chapter 12

# Death's Door

"Mrs. Johnson, come quickly!"

"What is wrong, Father?"

"It's Mr. Kennedy. He seems to be struggling to breathe."

"Mr. Kennedy, Mr. Kennedy, are you okay?"

After a few shakes by Mrs. Johnson, Mr. Kennedy suddenly yelled out, "Are you trying to kill me?"

"Mr. Kennedy, you scared me and Father Cruz."

"For crying out loud, don't either one of you know what a dead person looks like? I just took a quick power nap. I am not going to die until I finish my story. My boss has been trying to claim me for years, but God keeps interrupting his plan. Apparently, God, being so-called all-forgiving, is not ready to end the story. For me, it has been entertaining watching the constant battle between good and evil, and until the fat lady sings, it is not over.

"Where was I? Oh, yeah."

Now with my long-awaited wish finally granted, I was back in the house of my deceased parents. Trust me, it didn't look this good when I moved back in. After years of just sitting here with no occupants, it took hundreds of thousands of dollars to remodel it. Frankly, it was kind of funny.

On moving-in day, neighbors would come up to me, welcome, me and ask me my name. No one, absolutely no one, knew who I was. Everyone had either moved out or had died since my parents' accident. No one even remembered the accident or the scandal floating around church before the accident.

This was perfect! I was now a total stranger in my own house.

"Ed, can I interrupt?"

"Go ahead, but if I die before the end of the story, it's on your conscience."

"Fine, I take that chance. What was the outcome of your conversation with Edward? Where is he? What did the company give you? Did you ever get the actual name of his company? What happened with the FBI?"

"Cruz, my main man, they are all good questions. The best way for me to answer is start this way. The company name was Procnatas Inc."

"Procnatas Inc? What kind of name is that?"

"Well, Father, it is a name that describes 100 percent of their works and the final destination of all its followers who are unwilling to change."

"I don't understand."

"Father, in your spare time as a priest, do you ever do games like word jumbles or word scrambles?"

"No, not really."

"Is anything going to be easy with you? Look, on your own time, just move the letters of the company name around and see what shakes out. Solve that puzzle, and a lot of the story will make more sense. If you can't figure it out, take it to your Diocese's Vicar General for Divine Inspiration."

After all the crap I put up with dealing with Edward plus all the issues we were going to face from the FBI, I had big needs. I wanted respect, protection, money, power, or I could not guarantee my mouth would remain closed.

Honestly, it was pretty easy. Edward, his boss, and the company knew exactly what I was looking for. So the bottom line was we negotiated. I got what I wanted, and Edward got what he wanted, and we parted ways. That too was easy because no one in NY knew who we were or what we looked like.

Over the years, Edward and I kept the communication to a minimum. We never talked over the phone and hardly ever saw each other. Again, I got what I wanted, and he got what he wanted. Being social buds or best friends was never part of the deal, and frankly, it would have been risky.

Once the FBI started to dig and interrogate everyone associated with the company, it was not safe or, for that matter, very healthy to know too much. The investigations went on for years with the FBI poking and prodding Edward to the point that he would disappear for weeks at a time. I can only assume he was away on private company business trying to grow its foundation.

"Okay, Ed, that explains part of what happened to Edward, but what did you get from the company?"

"Me? Peace and a chance to reconcile."

"Reconcile? What does that mean? Reconcile with whom?"

"Wow, Father, you are just loaded with good questions. To me, *reconciliation* is such a complicated word. I lived a life in which I did many things that might be considered upsetting and disappointing to some and yet admired by others. Reconciling—or more simply put, asking forgiveness—is not always easy to do.

"With pride and free will, we all make choices. Some do not consider the consequences of their choice, and some don't care about the consequences. Others make bad choices during their life, and for whatever reason, they realize the error of their ways and change their life for the better. Call it divine inspiration or fire insurance against suffering the unknown. Who really knows what happens after death?

"Let me take Edward as an example. I just explained the errors of his ways throughout this entire story. Father, now let me ask you a question: do you believe if Edward was truly repentant for his poor decisions and if there was a heaven and hell, do you believe he could be saved?"

"If Edward was in the state of grace at the time of his death, yes, I believe he would be forgiven and saved."

"What if Edward, just before he died, told a little white lie to protect a secret that could endanger the lives of many people, including himself? Would he still be forgiven?"

"That is more difficult, but yes, I believe God, who is all loving, would forgive him."

"Today, to get forgiveness, does one have to say any special words to demonstrate sorrow to achieve forgiveness?"

"Ed, what is necessary is true sorrow for their sins and an open heart while asking God for forgiveness. Why are you asking me all these questions?"

"Well, Father, I guess my main reason is to see in today's world how you feel about the sacrament of reconciliation and to better understand how forgiveness is achieved in the eyes of God and His modern church. Remember, it has been a very long time since I heard the word *penance*, no less reconciliation."

"Naturally, Ed, is it safe to assume this is all about the status of Edward's soul? Am I correct?"

"Absolutely, Father Cruz. Who else would I be asking about?"

"Speaking of Edward, whatever happened to him and the ciborium?"

"That is another good question. I told you we all make choices, and Edward made his. I also told you when the company becomes unhappy with the commitment or lack of commitment within its leadership, things change.

"The rumor that has been circulating around for years is that Edward, once he moved back to Jamaica Estates, his company leadership became questionable. His interviews with the FBI did not stand up under heavy heat. It was almost like he was not himself. He fumbled with details and basically left the FBI asking more questions about the company. He could no longer protect the company, so his fate was sealed.

"Story has it on a trip to Haiti his plane disappeared without a trace, just like his parents'. It was a very sad and tragic choice and consequence by Edward."

"I am sorry, Ed. That is truly a terrible ending. With that sudden ending to his life, I can see why you would be concerned about his final resting place. Do you know what happened to the ciborium?"

"Listen, Father, I am very tired. Would you mind a short break? I need to close my eyes for fifteen minutes, then I promise I will wrap this whole story up."

"Fine, Ed, but can you at least answer the question what happened to the ciborium?"

"Yes, I can, and I will get to that shortly. Mrs. Johnson, please give Father a drink or whatever he desires, and something to eat. Wake me up in fifteen minutes. Thank you."

Father Cruz turned to Mrs. Johnson. "So, Mrs. Johnson, Mr. Kennedy is quite the storyteller."

"Sorry, Father, I don't know what you mean. I have been here for hours listening to his story—you know, his bait story. Father, I know nothing about the details of his story other than what Mr. Kennedy said to tell you and Mrs. Flannigan on the phone."

"You are telling me you have absolutely no idea about his story?"

"Correct, Father."

"He has never mentioned one word to you about his past. Correct Father, not one word? And the reason you called is because you had a feeling his soul was restless and he needed confession?"

"Yes, Father, that is accurate."

"Please, God, I hope he lasts through his nap. I still have no idea why I am here." Father Cruz paused. "What is that sweet aroma, Mrs. Johnson?"

"It has been here for years, but the cleaning service could never explain it. Father, since you have been here, I did notice it *is* getting stronger. Father, what would you like?"

"A cup of coffee would be great, Mrs. Johnson."

"Coming right up, Father. How about something to eat?"

"No thanks, coffee will be fine. Mrs. Johnson, did you know the Kennedy family before you took this job?"

"No, not really."

"Did you ever hear about a murder at our parish?"

"A murder? Never! I heard a Monsignor fell and died in the rectory years ago. No one ever said it was murder."

"Mrs. Johnson, I am not saying there was a murder. I am just asking if you ever heard of a murder in the parish."

"No, Father, I would remember something like that happening."

"How about a theft or a breaking into the tabernacle?"

"Father, where are you getting this stuff from? If Mr. Kennedy is telling you that kind of stuff, he is all messed up with medication. Don't believe anything he tells you. He makes up stuff all the time, and then a week later he doesn't remember he said it.

"I remember once he started telling me about seeing angels, and when I asked for more details, he said forget it, he was dreaming. I will have to admit when he was telling the story he did sound very convincing."

"What about relatives or companies he may have been associated with?"

"No, never a word."

"Again, tell me what made you decide to call me."

"I just had a feeling that Mr. Kennedy needed a priest. When I think about the moment that I decided to call the office, I get the chills, like the Holy Spirit was encouraging me to make the call."

"Did Mr. Kennedy discourage you about making the call?"

"No, he just never believed you would show up."

"There is that aroma again."

"Father, it is my coffee you smell. I make a strong cup of coffee. Can I get you a piece of cake or something?"

"No thanks, Mrs. Johnson. I am anxious to have Mr. Kennedy wake up so he can finish his bedtime story and I can really find out why I am here. Are you sure that aroma is your coffee? It smells unbelievably sweet to be a plain roasted coffee. Is that a flavored coffee?"

"Father Cruz, Mrs. Johnson, please come in here," Mr. Kennedy called out.

"Be right there, Mr. Kennedy. Thank you, Mrs. Johnson. Please know whatever feeling or inspiration made you call for a priest, you did the right thing. It has been my pleasure supporting your feelings and this parish. Thanks again for the coffee."

Father Cruz went to Mr. Kennedy.

"Okay, Father Cruz, I just gave you fifteen minutes to talk to Mrs. Johnson to check out my story. Did you find out anything to confirm what I have been telling you?"

"Mr. Kennedy, what makes you think I would talk to Mrs. Johnson?"

"Because you are a priest, and naturally, after what I have said about a murder, the bishop, a missing bowl of consecrated hosts, and so on and so forth, you would have to be dumb not to try to confirm all the facts. If I croak before you get proof and you know the story but have no proof, how could you protect the church in the event someone else brought my story to light? That would be bad for you. Like the bishop, you would have to lie, say you know nothing or continue the cover-up, taking it to your grave."

"She had no idea what you have been talking about. Furthermore, she basically said you're nuts."

"Nuts? We shall see about that. I need to get back to the teachings and beliefs of the church. Does the church still perform what we use to call 'last rites'?"

"Yes, but it is now known as the Anointing of the Sick."

"What sick? I'm dying! What if I die before I get your anointing?"

"Is that why I am here? Do you want the Anointing of the Sick sacrament?"

"In truth, Father, that remains to be seen."

"Ed, why do you say that? I would be happy to hear your confession and anoint you."

"What makes you think you have not already heard my confession?"

"Okay, Ed, now I am really confused."

"Mrs. Johnson, come in here, please!"

"Yes, Mr. Kennedy?"

"Go over to my closet, and get the big hatbox on the top shelf. Be careful, I don't want anything crushed."

"Ed, what is going on?" Father Cruz asked.

"Will you ever get patience, Cruz? Mrs. Johnson, bring the box over here, and set it on the bed." Mr. Kennedy turned to the priest. "Father, I am going to make a deal with you. I will give you all the proof you need and a witness besides. Mrs. Johnson, please stay here with me and Father for a minute. Father, you must promise me that when I pass on you will pray for me and undo the injustice that has been done to Jesus. You are a good priest sent to me by the divine intervention of God himself.

"Mrs. Johnson, I thank you for doing something that you will never comprehend. Furthermore, don't be frustrated as my witness, for you will never know the truth of this moment. Why? Because with the Sacrament of Reconciliation, Father has taken an oath of silence.

"Mrs. Johnson, please give me the box. Father, before I open the box, I am asking you to grant me the last rites. I have given you my confession, and now I give you the proof."

"Ed, besides your third-party story, I am not sure what confession you made."

"Well, Father, you know that little white lie we discussed?" With that, Ed opened the box. Upon opening the box, they all saw a big beautiful cowboy hat.

"Father, the anointing prayer, please."

As Father Cruz performed the last rites, granting absolution, Ed lifted the hat and softly said, "Father, I am not Ed Kennedy. My real name is Edward Flynn."

With that, he revealed the ciborium.

With the lid lifted, they found the aroma was truly divine.

Extracting one of the hosts out of the ciborium, Father Cruz gave it to Edward.

This time, all the hosts remained in sight, unchanged and protected for the past sixty years.

"Glorious Father, I am sorry for my sins. Thank you for your forgiveness!"

With that, Edward Flynn expired.

"Father Cruz," Mrs. Johnson spoke up.

"Yes, Mrs. Johnson?"

"Who was the Father he was talking about?"

"Mrs. Johnson, there is only one true Glorious Father."

# About the Author

Edward N. Kelley was born in Queens, New York. His struggles as a teen with low-level education led him to a life of juvenile delinquency, pool hustling, and menial jobs. A series of unexpected events began to change his outlook on life, and a chance meeting with a special woman resulted in forty-seven years of marriage to date. His family now includes two grown and married sons and three grandchildren.

Edward holds college degrees in aircraft electronics and electrical engineering, and has fifty years of work experience, including thirty years of corporate life and twenty years of demonstrating a private entrepreneurial spirit.

Presently living in Florida, Edward is now retired, pursuing his dream as a published author.

To date the author has released two inspirational autobiographies: *Under God's Plan: The Battle of Free Will* and *Tough to Forgive: A Darkened Soul*. This book, *The Missing Presence*, is his first fictional writing.

CPSIA information can be obtained
at www.ICGtesting.com
Printed in the USA
BVOW08s1450301117
501434BV00002B/68/P

9 781640 799745